OPERATION
Woman in Black

Rene Natan

PublishAmerica
Baltimore

First printing

ISBN: 1-4137-8365-1
PUBLISHED BY PUBLISHAMERICA, LLLP
www.publishamerica.com
Baltimore

Printed in the United States of America

*Dedicated to all parents of handicapped children,
especially Janey and Hugh Campbell,
who spare no efforts to bring joy to their child, Myles*

PART 1

1

Chief Detective Conrad Miguel Tormez leafed through the pictures taken at the scene of the accident. A beautiful woman lay inert in the driver's seat of a Corvette, seemingly asleep, her head reclined to one side. Her injuries had been all internal; there was not one single drop of blood on her body or in the car. Clara Moffatt had missed a curve, slid on the icy road, and capsized into the nearby creek.

Conrad looked at each of the pictures again. *What a waste,* he thought.

It had taken him two days to discover who she really was, where she was heading, and what she was up to. He was ready to file away the dossier he had in his hands, when a sudden idea crossed his mind.

Maybe her death could be put to good use.

Conrad paced his office in big strides, as a daring idea took shape in his mind. From time to time he stopped in front of the window, watching the bulldozer remove the last load of debris of what was once an elementary school. On that property a new wing of police headquarters was being erected to house a forensic laboratory. *A new office, new investigative tools and a recent promotion!* Conrad should be happy—but he wasn't. For the last few years the town of Varlee had been plagued with blackmail, its people spied on, their private lives exposed to scorn. Afraid of being demoted the previous Chief had resigned, and Conrad had taken charge of the on-going investigation.

After a few more strides, Conrad concluded that his idea was daring and unorthodox but do-able. He had to rely on his long-term friendship with Denis Taillard—and Denis had personal reasons to be part of the operation he had in mind.

7

An hour later a blond man in his early forties walked into his office.

"Let me do the talking," said Conrad Miguel Tormez to him. "What we're going to ask of Savina is hard—hard and dangerous. Her reaction may not be too positive." He grinned at his understatement. "Let me handle the situation. You just be charming. You have no problem with that when a woman is around, right?" He invited the handsome man standing in front of him to sit down. "But most important of all," he said, finishing his monologue, "don't get upset no matter what she says or does."

The man was ready to reply, when a tall, slim young woman in a blue uniform entered the room.

"Here I am, Mr. Tormez. Your message sounded urgent. I hope nothing's wrong with you." She took off her blue cap and shook her long, wavy hair.

"No. Thank you for your concern, Savina. Mr. Denis Taillard, Ms. Savina Thompson."

Denis rose and exchanged greetings with Savina. He was still holding her hand when Conrad gestured toward the coffee table near the window. "Let's sit comfortably," he said, smiling at Savina and at Denis in turn, his sparkling white teeth contrasting with his dark complexion. "Finally I have an office big enough for all my needs," he added, slumping into an armchair.

A tapestry of file cabinets covered the lower portion of the walls. On the desk a stack of papers competed for space with binders of varying thickness, size, and color. The workstation on the far left was dotted with yellow post-its. The presence of a telephone could only be guessed by the shape of the loose paper floating on top of it.

"Your office is nice and big," said Savina, twisting the ends of her long hair. "But I'm sure you didn't summon me so early in the morning just to admire it."

"Right. I'll come to that," he said slowly. "But, first, let me make sure Mr. Taillard and yourself become acquainted with each other."

"Well," said Denis smiling at Savina. "I already know a lot of nice things about Ms. Thompson."

Conrad ignored him. "Savina went through our school. After graduation she decided to accept the job of a security guard at a department store on Queens Quay, in downtown Toronto. Not as challenging as police work, she said, but she would be on duty mostly

8

during the day. Right?" He did not wait for an answer and continued, "Savina likes to play in amateur theaters. So being free at night is important to her." Conrad glanced at Savina's fingers. "Still unattached?" he asked, casually.

"Yes." She was clearly growing impatient, crossing and twisting her fingers. "But you didn't ask me here for that either, I don't think...."

"Right again," replied Conrad. "Matchmaking isn't my specialty." *Not as a rule*, he thought. "The police have a serious problem; I have a serious problem; Mr. Taillard has a serious problem. The reason I asked you here is because I believe that you, Savina, can help us all." The phone rang and Conrad rose to grab it. "Excuse me for a moment," he said.

Conrad's partial retreat made Denis and Savina aware of each other's presence.

"Conrad thinks the world of you," Denis said, moving to sit close to Savina. "I never heard him speak so highly of anyone."

Savina gave him a long, warm smile. "Do you know Conrad well, Mr. Taillard?"

"Yes. We practically grew up together. Call me Denis, please."

Conrad moved back and stood close to Savina, interrupting the exchange of words and smiles. He took the stage with his powerful voice. "Mr. Taillard is the owner of the Bergeron & Taillard Company—they manufacture sporting goods." He looked at Savina. "Oh, I was forgetting...I'd like you to keep what I'm going to say in the strictest confidence, Savina."

"Yes, Uncle."

"Good. I know I can count on you." He patted Savina on the shoulder and went to sit in the chair vacated by Denis. "Years back, when her parents died, I took Savina and her brother under my wing—they called me Uncle." Conrad continued, "So let's go back to our problem...like a few other wealthy businessmen in town, Mr. Taillard has been singled out for possible extortion. The idea is to lure people into sex scandals." He paused. "This time we have a lead on one of the perpetrators. We came across several messages that a recent employee of the Bergeron & Taillard Company had been receiving. For the moment, let's refer to this employee as the *Woman in Black*. She was in possession of a set of instructions to induce Mr.

Taillard into sex acts and tape them to embarrass him and possibly blackmail him. The woman, an old police acquaintance in another province, lived in a condominium located in the most expensive part of town. She assumed the appearance of a wealthy woman who works for having something to do, not for need. In other words, the kind of person in which Mr. Taillard would be interested."

"I see." Savina gave Denis a quizzical look. "Mr. Taillard is not married?"

"Not any more, but the crooks don't know it yet. I'll explain that later." Conrad rose to his feet and paced the room. "Clara Moffatt, the Woman in Black, died in a car accident three days ago. We found cameras, tapes, and other material in her car and apartment. We decided not to make her death public. Nobody claimed her body or showed up to declare her missing. From notes and phone calls on her machine we learned a great deal about the business she was in." Conrad was looking at Savina, who was busy observing Denis.

"Do you get the picture? We've a hook into an operation that escaped our investigation for years. One of the businessmen who didn't cooperate died. We weren't able to protect the other from damaging publicity after he'd reported the extortion attempt."

Conrad moved to a corner of his office and came back with coffee for everybody. He took a sip. He stood in front of Savina, conscious of dominating her with his six feet of height and two hundred pounds of mass.

"Savina, the reason I asked you here is because I'd like you to impersonate the Woman in Black."

Savina jumped to her feet and erupted, "What?" Her eyes flickered from Denis to Conrad. "You must be crazy! Both of you!"

"Just a moment, Savina. Let me elaborate."

Denis quickly cut in, "You've no obligation to do it. Actually, I don't expect you to do anything. It wasn't my idea. I believe it's dangerous and offensive to you as a person. It's my problem and a police matter—nothing to do with a nice girl like you."

Conrad made an effort to conceal his dismay. Denis shouldn't have beeped. He was trying to mount a difficult operation; he needed support, not contradictions! But he knew Savina would listen. She owed him big time.

After pacing the room, Savina sat down and Conrad continued. "First, let me tell you why Mr. Taillard is interested in cooperating. One of the two victims of this scam was the director of his firm and his closest friend. Mr. Taillard is as anxious as I am to break this criminal ring."

Savina did not answer. She only blinked nervously.

"Let me now explain what I'd like you to do. First, you've won a big lottery prize—a trip around the world! So you get a leave from your job." Conrad moved briskly to his desk. With one single move he fished, from underneath a stack of documents, a folder with a few pictures of Clara Moffatt. He displayed them on the coffee table.

Savina, however, kept looking at her interlocutors, an expression of disbelief clearly painted on her face.

"Second, you become the Woman in Black: medium-length blond hair, black clothes, and black accessories. Third, you wear brown contact lenses to change the color of your eyes. Fourth, you move into her place. Your figure, height, and weight are very close to hers. I don't know anybody who'd fit into that role better than you do."

"Great," said Savina ironically. "I think I should consider myself fortunate." There was a moment of embarrassing silence. "How long did you meditate this spoof?" Savina asked. "It seems you already figured out all the details."

"Not even thirty-six hours." Conrad continued. "For my idea to work, we have to move fast. Your part will last five, six weeks. We'll protect you all the way through."

"Why that long?"

"We can make it shorter…." cut in Denis.

"No, our criminals study the victims to perfection: habits, movements, social contacts, and so on. They have pictures of all the important places where Mr. Taillard spends time. Only the outdoors of his home and country house, however. We've got to play it their way or they'll catch on pretty soon that our girl is not their girl."

"I didn't say I'd do it. By the way, why all the black clothing?"

Fast as lighting Conrad preceded Denis in answering. "A matter of personal taste, nothing more than that." He paused to take another sip of his coffee. "Savina, I know Denis well. He'll make your life the most pleasant possible. You'll make our lives much better. I wouldn't ask you if I really could avoid it."

"So why six weeks?"

Conrad sighed. "That was the schedule we found in her planner…we have to follow it. Apparently she didn't want to give the impression of a cheap acquaintance. She wanted to play the woman not inclined to have an affair with a married man, but at the same time, very much attracted by him. That's the profile our experts came up with." He slowly finished his coffee. "There is a meeting at the tennis club...."

"I'm not good at the game."

"Great. Probably Clara would have played the helpless girl, and got Denis to teach her."

Savina blurted, "I think you're both crazy. You'll never pull it off...and what you ask of me is twice as crazy."

Denis was twisting in his chair, squeezing the armrests nervously.

Conrad stopped in front of Savina. "Well, Mr. Taillard and I have to discuss some other matters. We'll leave you here alone for a few minutes. Think about the idea. For my plan to work, we have to act quickly. Starting now. If you refuse, you'll not hear a peep about it. Not now. Not ever."

"Thank you for listening. I really appreciate it," Denis said as he rose to follow Conrad out.

2

Conrad and Denis took a stroll around the building in silence. Denis sat on one of the rustic benches, exhausted. "I felt so embarrassed when you...you made the request," he said.

"I knew you would be. But your physical presence was indispensable for the success of the entire operation. I had little to work with to push Savina. I had to bank on the fact that you're an attractive man." Conrad sat close to him and winked. "I know her weaknesses."

"I don't think she'll accept," said Denis. "In addition to the awkwardness of the situation, I think she doesn't like me."

Conrad couldn't help smiling. "Don't be so pessimistic." He waved three fingers in front of Denis' face. "It took me three meetings to convince you of the idea, and three meals—breakfast at the country club, lunch at your sister's, and dinner at Amalfi's. No wonder I put on weight! Let's get to the point. Savina reacted better than you did. She didn't swear!" Conrad laughed. "I never heard you swearing before! Another good sign: she's upset. If she had dismissed the idea altogether, she wouldn't be upset. She would just say *no* and walk away."

"Conrad, the entire idea is absurd."

"I asked for some cooperation."

"Never heard that mimicking sexual acts is a form of cooperation the police expect from citizens."

"I'd have never asked anybody else but you and Savina. I wouldn't have the nerve."

"She'd be foolish to accept. She has no obligations. The mission is dangerous and, first impression, she detests me."

13

"She may have not too much liking for wealthy people, and the black stuff was of no help. Why do you like women to dress up like at a funeral?"

"It's a long story. To make it short, I dislike all those casual, multicolor outfits that women, especially young people, wear today. You can't find anything too wild in black. That makes it pleasant to my eyes."

"I see. Let's go back now."

Savina was looking out the big window carved in the middle of the largest wall.

"Well, Savina, you had some time to think it over. Do you need a bit more or do I have an answer?"

"First, spell out what I'll have to do, in detail."

"You'll move into Clara Moffatt's condo. Our crew will occupy a nearby vacant apartment to photograph and monitor everybody who enters the building. I don't expect anybody to show up; but if so, we may use that person as the successive lead to reach our men. You'll be free." He paused and cleared his throat. "Meanwhile you become Mr. Taillard's secretary at the new office we set up inside his house. Nobody at Bergeron & Taillard's main office will see Clara again. They didn't take pictures inside any of Denis' residences; so I'm confident that while working for him you're safe. You'll have to meet Mr. Taillard socially, starting with the sports center."

In spite of the look of animosity Savina shot at him, Conrad did not deter. "We can cover the possibility that they'll contact you and that you'll have to return a call. Over the phone we'll use a new system called *Pappa-pappa*. It's a speech-recognition and translation device. It transposes acoustically each phoneme; that is, each of the forty basic sounds of the language. It also imitates all the syllables that spoken English collapses into one single sound. We have enough words and phrases from the real Woman in Black to transpose your words into words spoken with her pitch—*in real time*. The other party shouldn't notice the substitution. We've tried the system in this specific case on several members of our department. They couldn't distinguish whether Pappa-pappa was speaking or the real Woman in Black was on the phone. I'm pretty sure that you can express yourself using common words—maybe speaking a little slowly—and the other party will hear your words as if they were pronounced by our lady." Conrad paused. It was hard to hide his satisfaction thinking of the possibilities Pappa-pappa offered. "Here comes the best part of all: since our station will be monitoring the system, any of us, if needed, will be able to answer the phone and talk like the Woman in Black."

Savina sighed and stroked her long, wavy hair. "What if I'm confronted?"

"We hope to be there." Conrad shot her a curious look. "However, if I remember correctly, you were one of the best students in my class at Aylmer College. I taught you everything there is to know."

Savina remained silent for a moment. "What do I have to do with Mr. Taillard?"

"You both have to agree on a good tape. Your face should never appear, and Mr. Taillard's body should be well exposed. No doubts about what you are supposed to be doing." Conrad paused. He couldn't avoid shooting a teasing look at both. "You don't have to do anything special, just fake the act. But the imitation should be…how should I say? Realistic? Convincing? You know what I mean."

"It sounds so embarrassing…." Savina was twisting her long hair.

"I understand, but you're both nice people, and according to my information neither is too shy." He paused again. "Mr. Taillard is a very nice person: calm, kind, and excellent company in any circumstance. I'm sure he'll be tactful with you, Savina."

"That's already a problem." Savina threw the last dart before surrendering. "I like my men immediate, passionate, and full of zest." She looked defiantly at Denis.

A puzzled Denis was about to respond, when Conrad quickly preceded him. "Let's give it a try…let's agree that either of you can walk out of the deal without any explanation." There was a pause. "The first thing you have to do, Savina, is to shop for black clothing, since there's only a coat in the closet. Clara's outfits were in the car when she had the accident. They were ruined beyond repair. You'll have to buy everything black, even the undergarments. Here's the list and some money." He gave her a captivating smile. "Pay cash."

* * *

The idea of Savina impersonating the Woman in Black worried Denis Taillard. Though he trusted Conrad's intuition and competence, he knew that he was going to face a number of problems. He would have to deal with a woman outside his environment, with different habits, behavior and social skills. It would require a great deal of patience and understanding. His mind was still reeling when Conrad called.

"Operation Woman in Black is on," Conrad shouted. "Savina has accepted! Come over to her place in an hour. She's bought a new wardrobe; she's cut and died her hair. We need your opinion. If everything is in order, we move her into Clara Moffatt's condo. We got her a black Corvette, the same model as Clara's. We're all set."

Conrad's positive attitude was definitely contagious. "I'll be there," Denis replied.

"Use a cab and be sure you aren't followed."

Denis approached Savina's apartment with mixed feelings: apprehension over the unusual situation, curiosity to see Savina in Clara's clothes, and pleasure at meeting Savina again.

The door of her apartment opened onto a living room furnished with an oval table, two wooden chairs, a china cabinet, and an old sofa. The windowsill was crammed with purple and white African violets. The place was small, but neat and cozy.

Denis walked in and sat on the sofa, close to Conrad.

Soon Savina made her appearance. Her straight blond hair swayed as she paraded in front of the two men. She wore a double-lapel suit, with only one big button at the front. Without a word, she walked to face Conrad, took one step sideways and stopped in front of Denis.

She turned around and let the wrap-around skirt fall to the floor, a small, lace slip revealing more than what it was supposed to conceal.

She definitely had great legs. "Nice show," said Denis. He peered at his companion. Conrad looked appalled.

But the show had just started. Savina unbuttoned the jacket and threw it on the floor, showing a lace bra and a slim, well-built body. She slowly turned around once more. Denis enjoyed the stunt, but Conrad did not dare look.

"Savina, please, you're almost naked," Conrad said, covering his eyes.

"I don't know if Mr. Taillard is turned on by black or natural-color stockings. That's why I look so naked."

"Natural color," Denis answered promptly. "The outfit looks beautiful on you and so does the lingerie." He wanted to give her credit for being a good sport.

"Next outfit, please," said Conrad hastily.

"But I still have five pieces of undergarments…."

"No lingerie and no stripping," Conrad hissed between his teeth.

The evening gown was straight, closed at the front, with a big V-slit at the back: Savina looked wonderful in it, only her walk was uncertain because of the high heels.

Denis gave her a hand. "You look very elegant," he said.

Conrad was still perspiring because of the first exhibition, when Savina showed up in a transparent black nightgown. The pleats unfolded from top to bottom. She was naked underneath, and that made Conrad explode.

"Go and change!"

"Why?" Savina was making a point. "I have to pose in the nude in front of a man who is a stranger to me in the spirit of duty and cooperation, and you—you can't look at a naked girl?" She stood in front of him and rollicked close to Denis.

"Does my shopping meet with your approval?"

Denis rose, took her hand and kissed it. "It surely does. Absolutely. Completely. Totally."

From the nearby table Savina picked up a piece of paper. She waved it in front of the two men. She said, "That's good, gentlemen, because here's the bill: six thousand, nine hundred and ninety-seven dollars."

When he entered Conrad's unmarked car, Denis was still laughing at Savina's performance. "Don't be upset," he said to his friend. "Savina let off some steam. She was entitled to it, after what we put her through. And she did it in a pleasant way. I truly enjoyed the show. You can't fault her for lack of humor."

"You may be right," Conrad replied quietly. "It's just that to me she is still the little girl I bounced up and down my knees."

"But you asked her to act in a grownup's role—and what a role! One no amateur actor would accept!" He gave Conrad a look. "You still didn't tell me why you thought she would accept. What are you holding on her?"

Conrad was about to answer when a raccoon jumped out of the ditch and stopped in the middle of the right lane, as if it were hypnotized by the car lights. Conrad swayed to the left to avoid it. "It's a long story. Her parents died at about the same time. They were shot with a .300 Magnum rifle, very near to my house. Her father, who at that time was my partner, died instantly. Her mother died a month later; she never recovered from the multiple wounds." Conrad paused. "You see, they'd borrowed my station wagon to take the kids to the beach. It was a long weekend, and I couldn't go anywhere, since I was on duty." Conrad stopped, pensive. "After so many years I still wonder if those shots were meant for me. We never found who did it; never even had a clue who the sniper was. Savina and her brother had to go to a home. Savina was fifteen, the boy not even ten.

"When Savina started to earn money, she took her brother with her. The boy wasn't the brightest kid in the neighborhood. They used him to deliver drugs. He was caught. It was a difficult moment for Savina. I helped out. One offence was committed when the boy was a minor. The other a week after the boy turned eighteen." Conrad paused. "We dropped that one charge."

"I see," Denis said. "That why she felt obliged to comply with your request."

"I was counting on that, to be honest. But I wouldn't have held it against her, had she refused. It's just that we're stuck. This criminal ring is powerful. It has made several victims—the last being my boss. One theft after the other; then rumors that several industrialists each paid half a million dollars to avoid being exposed." Conrad paused. "Of course the last two cases finished him. Too much exposure: the media kept talking about them, hinting the police were inept. At first there were some useful clues, but those leads soon ran dry. My boss couldn't cope with the situation any more. He resigned." Conrad became pensive. "Maybe I'll have to give it up, too."

After a few minutes of silence, Denis asked, "Do you really think you can get away with Savina talking like Clara?"

"Yes. But Savina won't have to speak like Clara—that would take weeks of training. Our system will do that for her. Let me backtrack a bit and explain how Clara and her boss communicated with each other." Conrad cleared his throat as though to prepare for a long talk. "Her boss calls from a public phone—from what we know, located in Toronto—and leaves a message for Clara on her machine. What does Clara do? She calls her own phone number and leaves a message on her voice mail. Her boss has the password to access Clara's phone from any other phone in the country. He listens to what Clara has to say. Got the idea? Her boss is always in the clear; the only person who can be nailed is the phone's owner. We wouldn't know of this system, if Clara had erased the messages. But she didn't. So Clara's negligence in wiping out her old messages, combined with the fact that she never received any other calls, sparked the idea of the substitution." Conrad shot a look at Denis, who bobbed his head.

"Clara Moffatt never received a call she had to answer directly?" Denis asked.

"No, at least not according to the records in our possession. However, since this could happen now, we need a system that can match Savina's words with Clara's in *real time*."

"Got it," Denis said. "Not bad thinking. Quite smart, actually." The car stopped in front of Denis' house. He was already out of the car when he asked, "Isn't it dangerous for Savina?"

Conrad seemed to weigh his answer. "It is, because we don't really know what we're up against. Sometimes I feel that the mastermind of these scams knows me, and anticipates my moves. It's been a very frustrating situation." He sighed. "To start with, Savina knows police procedures. She'll follow them to the letter—I know her. Then I'll prepare some additional instructions. And I intend to lay them down in such a way that, no matter what the situation, she'll have a way out."

"I see. I'll try to make her life as pleasant as possible," Denis said. He closed the car door and waved Conrad goodbye.

3

On the northern shore of Lake Erie

From up to a hundred feet from the coast, the two cliffs appeared to be one. A narrow strait, however, allowed a boat about 20' wide to squeeze through. The nondescript boat reached a small, secluded bay. Kurt Todd jumped ashore and threw the rope around the dock's buoy. He swiftly headed toward the cliff. As he fingered a lizard-shaped stone, the doors of an elevator swung open. He entered it and rode up to street level. Through a tunnel he reached his headquarters. This was the place where he made major decisions, exchanged money, developed films, falsified documents, and faxed or emailed messages. A satellite dish, encased between two protruding rocks, was the only element that offered entertainment during his solitary stays. The street-level entrance, on the northern side of the cliff, was camouflaged like a mossy, rugged surface and opened and closed with a remote control. A movie camera, inserted into the external wall and well concealed from the outside by the branches of a pine tree, allowed Todd to keep under surveillance the immediate area outside.

There stood a shabby cottage, made of metal siding with a roof in urgent need of repair. A vegetable garden on one side and a playground on the other closed into each other, barely leaving room for a driveway. Kurt glanced around. The cottage owner, Fred Kusteroff, wasn't home since his cab wasn't in sight. Fred wasn't the smartest person on earth, but he was his most trustworthy man, ready to execute any order without hesitation.

Everything was quiet. Kurt retraced his steps and entered his office. He slumped into his chair, exhaling deeply.

A decade ago he had set up the perfect criminal ring; since then he had been running it as a modern business. He diversified his activities, and kept abreast of the latest techniques in telephone and computer communications. To function effectively he relied on people with different talents and only on himself to invest the fruits of his enterprises. Theft produced a steady income, even if only about a quarter million dollars a year. Blackmail was the most profitable activity and the system he and his girlfriend, Clara Moffatt, had engineered was successful—or at least it was until a few months ago. Clara approached a married man, wealthy of course, and made a play for him. After a few weeks of veiled seduction from the expert Clara, a weekend of fun and pleasure followed very naturally. Then an hour-long videotape recorded the encounter. At first the strong muscles of the man's shoulders or his back, bunch up, took most of the frames. But once the wave of passion was over, the man, exhausted, would turn around to lay flat on the bed, his body appearing in all its nudity, his identity unmistakably clear.

Such a tape easily produced a half million dollars, since the victims preferred paying to being exposed. The system had worked with ninety percent success until a few months ago. Then it had happened. Two high-profile businessmen had refused to comply with his demands. One had committed suicide, the other had gone straight to the police. For three consecutive weeks there were big headlines in the newspapers. Worst of all, the material he had previously mailed his victims had landed in the hands of the authorities; now they had a clue about his modus operandi. Conrad Tormez, the new Chief Detective and his mortal enemy, had probably spent days analyzing the pictures he had sent to his victims, having the envelopes tested for DNA in the saliva, and trying to determine what sort of printer had been used for the messages.

Todd sighed as he reached for the mug of cold coffee lying on his desk. He had spent hundreds of thousands of dollars to set up those operations, and all he had now was a ton of compromising material he had to dispose of.

He wondered if it was time to retire. He got a small mirror out of his desk drawer and appraised his reflected image. His gray hair was thick and his facial features were fine. At fifty-two, he was still an attractive man. Maybe he should retire, settle in a fancy place, and enjoy the wealth he had so far accumulated. Hmm…but what would he do all day? He loved challenge, even risk; he loved controlling people who depended on him for a living; he loved change and uncertainty—they made him feel alive. No, he wouldn't spend the remaining part of his life roasting on the beach, playing Black Jack or running after a stupid golf ball. He was born for action. A little setback should not throw him off. *After all he was Kurt Todd!*

He made himself a fresh cup of coffee and dialed Clara Moffatt's number, hoping to get some news on her whereabouts. Clara was involved in the Taillard's operation. Together they had targeted Denis Taillard as their next victim and Clara had had no difficulties in getting close to him. Things were going as planned, when Clara had to rush to Berry to see her dying mother. That was the last message she had left on her recording machine, days back.

When an operation was on the go they avoided leaving tracks of their doing: no meetings, no two-way communications; only recorded messages which would let each other know what was important while appearing natural and anonymous.

After the first ring Clara's voice resounded nice and clear. "Sorry folks I didn't reply to your messages. Unfortunately I have sad news. My mother passed away. I got very busy with all the funeral arrangements. I'm back to work now. Talk to you soon. Bye-bye."

Kurt breathed with relief. Clara was okay. She would soon take care of the last phase of the Taillard's operation. He just had to be patient. Then Clara would be back and another half million dollars would be added to his captial.

He rose and began pacing his office, maneuvering among the furniture and the equipment that clogged the small area. He neared the hole he had carved in the stony wall to get a view of Lake Erie. Big waves with white ruffles raked the dark waters, seemingly hurrying to come to shore. It was windy, very windy. He would have to wait to use the incinerator to dispose of the compromising material he had so far accumulated.

4

Norman Arbib knew the situation was dramatic. A year ago he had misplaced a stamp valued at more than twenty-five thousand dollars and he had not been able to trace it back. His boss, Kurt Todd, would not put the matter to rest. He had punished him unrelentingly, making him do all sorts of miserable jobs: cleaning his rocky refuge, polish his boat to a shine in the middle of winter, transporting material to the new house Todd was building miles away, and hiding surveillance equipment amidst the shrubs surrounding The Hermitage, a fancy resort area east of Toronto. *I should find a way to spring free from such an obsessive man without pissing him off,* Norman thought. Too late he had discovered that he wasn't born to be a hard criminal. He didn't mind a little cheating here and there or telling stories to obtain what he wanted, but living dangerously was not in his make. He was pushing thirty now and began dreaming of settling down and having a steady job.

But his dream would not come true until he found that damned stamp. He got into his car, an old Chevrolet Caprice, and drove. He was only twenty miles from Todd's refuge when a signed advised, *Be ready to stop.* An ambulance passed him at great speed, followed, a few minutes later, by two tow trucks. *An accident!* Then contorted metal pieces appeared on the road. Traffic stopped.

Norman turned off the engine and sighed. He was going to be late. Todd would be furious, but there was nothing he could do. He reclined his head over the steering wheel as his mind went back to that fatal day in April, the day he got busted.

He had lingered all afternoon at the Toronto railway station waiting for his contact to show up. In his pocket he carried a

23

collector's item, a stamp known as the *Gronchi Rosa*. He was supposed to exchange it for $26,000. Norman had scrutinized all passengers getting off the last train. Only when all stands and wickets closed had he left, leaving behind a totally deserted station.

Todd's orders were to return to the south shore with the boat docked at the nearby marina. On his way to the Canadian shore Norman had carefully punched into the Loran-C the coordinates needed to reach the other side of the lake safely, avoiding all obstacles from buoys to fishing nets. In principle, the boat would have been able to return on its own.

But even as a kid Norman was afraid of water more than anything else. When he looked around, he saw a blanket of thick fog spreading over the entire harbor. It wasn't safe to go on the lake in those conditions. It'd be better to spend the night at the Royal York Hotel across the street.

He still remembered how nervous he was when he opened the heavy door and cautiously crossed the hotel hall. He was heading to the second floor when his cellular rang: his contact had been arrested and the police were looking for him. Norman looked around. The hotel's largest reception hall, the Victoria, was wide open in front of him with a big banner on top of the entry that read: *The Friends of Austria: Annual Party.*

From the other end of the long corridor two policemen advanced toward him, their stride fast and firm.

His stomach churned. With two quick steps Norman crossed the threshold and entered the hall. His decision was swift and final: he would unload the Gronchi Rosa.

Standing close to him was a tall girl in a red outfit. With an unnoticeable gesture Norman freed the precious stamp of its flimsy envelope, and slid it into her suit pocket.

Did she ever find it and, if so, what did she do with it? And who was that girl? So far all the searches had not produced any useful leads.

A knock on his car window signaled him he had to move. One lane had been cleared and the traffic moved, even if only in alternate fashion. Soon after Norman reached Todd's fancy hideout.

His boss looked tall even when he sat behind his desk. He stared at Norman first, then shot him a look full of contempt.

Norman sustained Todd's icy glaze, standing erect in front of him. After all Todd needed him, now that two operations had failed, and one of his men, actively hounded by police, had to go into hiding in the Rocky Mountains. Norman calmly repeated the old story again about the stamp. "They would have found it, I assure you. They stripped me of all my clothes, cut all the linings, and sliced my shoes as if to prepare them for a stir-fry. They searched every cavity in my body. If I hadn't unloaded it, they'd have found it, I guarantee you." He stopped hoping to have convinced his boss. He didn't look any more sympathetic now than when he had told him of his arrest the first time. "We still have a chance to recover it," Norman added in an undertone.

"You've had more than a year to find it," Todd said, and rose. "I'll give you an extra thirty days to get it back." He gave him a look that promised the worst. "After that, you'll have to start digging the tunnel for my big house." He laughed his usual brief, jittery laughter. He walked toward the door and clicked on the remote to open it. He gestured him out and said, "And don't try to take off. I'll find you no matter where you hide."

Todd sat in his chair and swiveled to face the TV screen. Time to watch the news.

"Found at last," was the big announcement. "The wreckage of the Simpsons' plane is currently being searched." The plane had disappeared two weeks ago and poor meteorological conditions had slowed down the search. The rescue workers, in their bright orange coats with green stripes on the backs, were frantically digging in the snow, the wind seemingly blowing from all sides. Kurt could hardly see what was happening. But in no time the pilot's body was pulled out of a Cherokee Piper. A short intermission from the live show allowed the broadcast of the international news, but soon the cameras focused on the rescue team again. Mr. Simpson's body had been found a few feet away from the plane with his briefcase. The team was still searching for Mrs. Simpson and her child, the anchorman reported. The darkness of the incipient night would not allow the operation to continue, he announced soon after.

Kurt Todd's eyes were glued to the screen. A few moments later a brief report on the Simpson family followed.

Months before Mr. Simpson had suffered a major financial setback. In spite of several attempts to inject new money into his construction company, he'd had to declare bankruptcy. He was on his way to Edmonton to visit his uncle when the accident occurred. So far, there was no reason to doubt the crash was due to poor weather conditions. Mount Maudit, always attracting the thickest clouds, had been once again par to its name.

Kurt Todd had no interest in the Simpsons or their story. Unfortunately all the rescue activities took place around Barnist, a village in the Rockies very close to where one of his men was in hiding. He could only hope that Al Garnett was sensible enough to keep a low profile.

5

Conrad had not eaten all day. Nobody was waiting for him at home, so it would have made sense to stop at a restaurant and have supper. But after a long day of hassles and troubles, going home had a particular meaning for him, recoiling into his castle, to the place he could call his own and where no stranger could intrude, to the place that once had been full of life and joy.

Conrad parked his car and walked to the front of the house. He turned on the décor light fixtures near the main entrance and dusted off the snow from the storm door.

Built on a rise, with old red bricks and white trim, the house had been the dream come true of his late wife, Sharon. She had planted trees, bushes and perennials at the front and dug a little pond in one corner of the backyard. She had made it a home and filled it with laughter and love.

Conrad entered the house and followed the hallway that streamed into the living room. The carpet, once a vivid green, had faded to a dull gray; the oblong coffee table showed scars of glasses carelessly deposited. On the credenza two candlesticks held their tapers burned down—a souvenir of the last anniversary Sharon and Conrad had celebrated.

Wallowing in his memories, Conrad did not move when he first heard the trill of the phone. Then with a large stride, he reached for it. "Yes," he said as he untangled the cord, "Yes, this is Conrad Tormez." He listened. "Are you sure?" he shouted into the mouthpiece, incredulous. He listened some more. "She won't leave, in spite of the cold weather? Is she okay?"

Excited, Conrad jerked the phone cord up and down. "Of course I'll come down. Be there tomorrow!" he shouted. He put the phone back in its cradle. For a moment he did not move, he couldn't believe what he had just been told. The prayer he'd addressed to the Almighty night after night had been heard and the only wish he had left in his heart granted. While looking for a missing plane near the foot of Mount Maudit, they had found his beloved daughter, Isabel, now fifteen years old. She was well, he had been told, and tomorrow he would cradle her in his arms.

"Wonderful!" he shouted. He stood in front of the big birdcage, where Isabel's pets were scratching their beaks on a limestone. "They've found her," he announced to the two canaries. "She'll soon be back to take care of you."

He began pacing the room, his mind reliving the time he had seen last Isabel, more than a year ago.

It was at a summer camp for youngsters with disabilities. Prone on the grass, Isabel had spent the entire afternoon showing him the wild flowers she had collected and carefully pasted on the pages of an album. She looked happy and much alive, the body of a young woman, the mind of a child.

Soon after, tragedy had struck. After a swim in the lake, Isabel couldn't be accounted for. Dozens of volunteers had been dispersed on land, and professional divers in the water. But they couldn't find any trace of Isabel. Then the cold weather had set in, halting all efforts and damping all hopes. Conrad, however, had never stopped looking for her, following every lead, even the faintest of all. And now…he wondered what had really happened. He would find out—with time, though, since Isabel suffered of frequent memory lapses.

Conrad glanced at a family picture standing on the side table. Sharon held baby Isabel in her arms, a big smile on her face. The little girl meant so much to her…Sharon had waited twelve years for that child. And when Isabel was finally born, Sharon became the happiest person in the country. Endless times she counted her fingers, kissed them, and caressed the dark fuzz on Isabel's head.

Conrad sighed.

He remembered the day Isabel got sick. At the hospital they didn't know what had caused it, and they had no way to help the child. And when Isabel got better, she talked in spurts; her memory seemed to be selective and short-term; her movements had become fast but uncoordinated, often jerky.

Sharon became withdrawn and sadder every day that went by.

She died before Isabel's full status of retardation could be assessed.

With a double squeak the side door opened and closed, breaking Conrad's reverie. "A tisane or a drink?" a voice from the kitchen asked.

"Drinks tonight, Bernice!" Conrad replied, his voice a high pitch. Bernice Berstow was his neighbor and long-time friend. "We're going to celebrate!" He quickened his steps as he walked into the kitchen and took hold of Bernice's arms. "You won't believe this: they have found Isabel!"

Startled, Bernice replied, "Oh, my God. Is she well?"

"Apparently yes. They're going to drop off a couple of faxes later tonight. I'll be able to see how she looks myself. I'll be flying to Barnist tomorrow morning. I hope I can take her home right away." Conrad paused. "However, I'd have to be careful. I don't want to distress her." He took Bernice's hand and led her into the family room. "Let's celebrate in style. I'll open a bottle of that champagne you gave me for my birthday. Why don't you prepare some snacks to go with it? I'm famished."

6

Saw-tooth mountains appeared and disappeared on the horizon as clear skies gave way to clusters of clouds. Conrad nervously shuffled the new faxes he held in his hands. They were pictures of a log cabin surrounded by bushes and trees, except for a clearing in front of the entrance. How in the world had his dear Isabel ended up in a place like that? Did she suffer, confined in such a secluded place? Conrad set the pictures aside and looked out of the small window. Mount Maudit had made its sinister appearance. Its top was dark gray; a huge glacier covered most of the front part; and the sides were nothing but sharp, steep cliffs. When the chopper entered a narrow valley, the miniscule village of Barnist drifted into sight. The chopper flew along the valley for a few miles and began the descent.

"Are you sure she has a baby with her?" Conrad asked the Mountie for the second time.

In a calm undertone the man replied, "Yes, and a dog, kind of." He shifted in his seat that was far too small for his size. As Conrad turned around to shoot him one of his famous dirty looks, he added, "It's a gray wolf, Sir."

Conrad sighed. He definitely had to see it.

The chopper maneuvered for landing. "What the hell...?" Conrad hissed, staring into the distance. "There's a chopper heading our way. I thought this was going to be a private affair." He turned toward Rudy Ashwald. "Can you read what's written on the side?" Constable Ashwald's eyesight was better than an eagle's.

"I can't read all of it. TV station, maybe?" He blinked a couple of times. "Yes. Mountains View TV Station, Channel 5. I'm afraid there's a second one, Sir."

"Shit!" Conrad mumbled between his teeth.

30

The Mountie spoke, "Not much can be done. You heard of the plane, right? About the Simpson family wiped out in the crash?"

"Oh yes, I did," Conrad replied.

"The rescue teams are still looking for some members of the family. That's why reporters have flooded all nearby airports." The Mountie added, "Rudy and I will keep the crowd out of your way as much as possible."

"Thanks." But Conrad knew it wasn't going to be easy. "If you have problems, try an emotional appeal. Tell them I'd like to have a few moments alone with my daughter, if the young woman in the log house is indeed my daughter. When we come out, they can shoot all the pictures they want."

The helicopter touched ground. Conrad pushed the door wide and sprang out. The accumulation of snow, however, forced him to arch his legs high as he approached the cabin. On the left, drifting snow had already covered one wall; on the right a rustic cross marked a grave; smoke whirled out of the chimney to quickly disperse in the air.

Conrad reached the house and stopped cold. After all, he wasn't prepared for the encounter. He cautiously opened the squeaky door and peeked inside.

Close to the fireplace a young woman was rocking a baby, the chair shrieking with each move. She turned her head as a drift of cold air invaded the room.

"Isabel!" Conrad cried. He moved to her, his arms ready for an embrace.

The girl rose, and with both arms she offered him an infant. As Conrad took him, she pointed at him and said, "He is my baby! My own!"

Conrad held the baby with one arm, and pulled Isabel close to his chest with the other. "My dear child," he murmured. "I found you! Alive and well!"

He buried his face in her hair to hide his tears.

When he finally was sure that his voice wouldn't betray his emotions, Conrad glanced at the baby. He seemed well fed and at ease. "Let's sit close to the fire," he said and looked around in search of chairs. The two in sight were buried under a multitude of clothing, plastic sheets and other unidentifiable objects.

Isabel sat on the rug in front of the fire and Conrad joined her, cradling the baby in his arms. "Tell me, Isabel, how have you been?"

"Good." Her fine hair captured the glow of the flames, giving her an angelic aura. "And this nice baby: does he keep you busy?"

"Yes." Isabel smiled. "I like him."

"I'm sure you do, my dear child. But isn't this place a bit strange?" There were logs around the fireplace and cans of food stuck on the shelves a few feet away. Isabel shrugged. *Of course, what a stupid question I asked!* Conrad thought. Isabel didn't understand what strange meant. And probably she hardly remembered their home in Varlee, since more than a year had gone by. "It's pretty nice and warm here. Did you start the fire yourself?"

Isabel nodded proudly. There was a soft bark and an insistent scratching at the door. "Oh, the dog!" she said and let the dog in. It was a beautiful wolf pup, four months old or so, Conrad guessed. Clearly from a late litter. Its gray fur took on shades of brown on the shoulders and the head. It wagged its tail festively as Isabel indulged in a long petting, then it sniffed around. As it spotted Conrad, it went to sit in the far corner of the large room. The Mountie was right. There was a wolf in the log house.

Isabel stretched near Conrad and put her head on his shoulder. "A story? Are you going to tell me a story?"

Conrad was surprised. The last time he had told her a story she was nine or ten. But then things were different with Isabel. Maybe this was her way to reconnect with her past. So he began, "Once upon the time there was a beautiful princess…."

The last log had burned, leaving only embers and ashes, at times revived by a draft sifting down the chimney. Outside, snow still fell. Conrad looked with apprehension at the small window, now completely covered with snow. He had to convince Isabel to leave with him, and soon.

Isabel knelt close to the crib and caressed the baby's head. "Isn't he beautiful? His name is Conrad Junior. He's a boy." The baby, asleep, did not make a sound.

"Conrad Junior, eh? He's beautiful, yes, like his mother." Conrad stretched his arm to stroke Isabel's long hair, then he rose, pushed the crib aside and sat close to his daughter. "He's healthy too. You took good care of him." How, Conrad couldn't figure out. "You've been a very good mother. But we want to be sure Junior has everything he needs in the future too, good food and warm clothes, right?"

Isabel bobbed her head. "You'll help us, eh, Dad?"

Conrad had not heard that word for more than a year. He dried a tear with the back of his hand; but more came, like a river. His voice catching in his throat, he mumbled, "Sure, sweetheart." He caressed her hair again. "Let's think what we should be doing. What about taking you and your baby to our old house? We could give Junior a room all to himself." Conrad waited to gauge her reaction, but there was none. "And a lot of toys, too!"

Isabel jumped to her feet. "Yes, yes, yes! Junior will be happy." She whirled around and flapped her arms.

Conrad continued, "And when he's older he can play in the swimming pool. That big yellow pool we installed for you." He wanted to take Isabel out of the cabin as soon as possible. The precipitation had intensified and the wind had gained strength; one chopper from the TV station had already left, and the others couldn't wait much longer.

Isabel threw her arms up. "Wonderful!"

Conrad rose. "And we could paint his room blue, since he's a boy, right?"

Isabel threw her arms around Conrad's neck. "Oh Dad, I'm so happy you came...."

Conrad held her tight for a long moment. Tears began gushing down his face again. He inhaled deeply. There was no time left for emotions; they had to leave. "Let's get ready. You get your coat and I'll wrap up Junior. We'll pick up all your stuff later."

7

Bernice Berstow had moved to Varlee with her son, Jerome, just after the death of her husband. She had been shopping for a house for two weeks straight, when she came across the house next to Conrad's. The owner had to move west in a hurry and wanted to unload the estate very quickly. The two-story home had been designed and built by an architect ready to retire. It was small and more than fifty years old with a steep brown roof, a mansard and two bay windows at the front that gave the building a very distinctive look. Bernice liked it at once and, after meeting some of the neighbors, she decided to buy it. The insurance money she had received for her husband's death, thirty-five thousand dollars, paid for the house. Her small pension provided for her and her son's needs. A big backyard, where she planted a big vegetable garden, kept her busy in the summer; in the bad season she knitted or quilted, the income from this activity nicely complementing her monthly pension.

As soon as she had settled in her new home Bernice took a liking to Isabel, who was then ten, and agreed to supervise her three afternoons a week. She involved Isabel in several different activities, making her feel useful. Soon Isabel became more alert and her speech more articulated. Bernice had her problems with her own son, however. After the death of his father, Jerome, just thirteen, often challenged her parental authority. Bernice found comfort and advice in Conrad, who played father to Jerome as a way to compensate Bernice for the loving assistance she gave to Isabel.

Isabel's disappearance hit Bernice hard, but it enhanced her friendship with Conrad. For a year Conrad had been thinking of asking her to marry him; he had waited for the right moment, when his job would allow him to take some time off. Unfortunately that wouldn't happen until a major breakthrough in the criminal ring that was plaguing Varlee occurred. And that was the major reason he had not proposed to her yet.

On his return from Barnist Conrad asked Bernice to look after Isabel while he rushed Junior to the doctor. The baby looked vital and healthy, but there was no way to know if he had gotten all the necessary shots. He anxiously waited for the doctor's response which, however, was very positive. They would wait for a few weeks, and then give him some booster shots. Relieved, Conrad drove home. The next problem he had to take care of was the wolf pup he had let free to roam in his backyard. When he arrived the pup wasn't there. A hole underneath the fence between his and Bernice's houses told him where to look. He picked up Junior and knocked on Bernice's door. The pup was there, sprawled underneath Isabel's chair.

Isabel jumped to her feet and grabbed the baby from Conrad's arms. She kissed him on both cheeks, a cheerful noise letting everybody know that the child was happy. Holding the baby high on her shoulder she began walking back and forth.

Bernice gestured Conrad to follow her into the kitchen. "I don't like the dog," she said. "It growls every time I get close to it."

"How did it get here?"

"It was in my backyard; it barked and Isabel let him in right away. She played with it for a long time while you were away. The dog doesn't want anybody else around."

Conrad nodded. "That's what I'd expect from a wolf pup," he said and slumped into a chair. "This morning I took the baby to the doctor." He told Bernice of the good news about Junior's health. "My next problem is to find a way to get rid of the wolf. I already talked about it to the station. It can be taken back where it came from, the big issue is Isabel. She's very attached to it, from what I can see."

"Yes. We shouldn't upset her, yet the presence of that pup is a threat for the baby."

The wolf pup had to go. In Barnist, just before the aircraft was going to withdraw the staircase, the animal had hopped in and gone to lie at Isabel's feet, all in one decisive, single yet smooth move. It was a superb creature: strong, alert, agile, and clearly committed to Isabel. Conrad wondered, *Even if her mind could not grasp things clearly, had*

Isabel perceived that strong bond, or was there another reason she was so attached to that pup? In any case, separating her from the wolf was not going to be easy. But there was danger, and that danger would increase as the pup grew. It had growled at Conrad when he grabbed it and confined it to the garage for the night. Every time he tried to convince Isabel that the creature was dangerous, she responded by shaking her head and raising her chin in defiance.

No use in doing any more talking: *it's time for action*, thought Conrad as he began driving. Within a few minutes he was at the Humane Society.

Free to roam, he looked at all the dogs available for adoption. None resembled the one Isabel had. He decided to go downtown and look in the *Make a Friend for Life* shop. He parked his car in a spot reserved for police vehicles and walked down Main Street. This was Varlee's fancy part of town, where shops flourished overnight and disappeared a few months later. He walked past a gift shop and a tiny bakery, from which the inviting smell of fresh muffins emanated. If it weren't so late, he would surely stop and taste one. While waiting for the green light at the crossing, he glanced at the newsstand. Together with the national press, *The Varlee Dispatch* displayed a big headline: *Conrad Tormez: A Happy Father, A Baffled Detective*. No need to read that story, he mused, since he was the one making it. He marveled at the ability reporters have to cut through skin and flesh, and knife you right in your guts.

He resumed his brisk walk, only to come to a sudden halt soon after. A white poodle majestically crossed his path, hardly concerned about its master still inside the pet-grooming shop and holding an extendable leash. Conrad looped around it and walked by the Art Gallery, where a big banner advertised the upcoming exhibition of Inuit sculptures.

Finally he reached the pet shop. In the front window two kittens played with yarn while a third lay on its back trying to untangle its paws from a thousand threads. Attracted by a soft barking, Conrad walked to the back of the shop where the dogs' cages were located, and opened one. A husky pup began licking his hands, clearly happy for the unexpected attention. Its gray coat, white muzzle, and clear eyes looked pretty much like the gray wolf's. It was small, however; probably only a month old. In a hurry to go home, Conrad didn't ask the price; he just took the critter to the cashier's counter.

"The puppies from that litter are simply adorable," the shop owner, a woman in her forties, said. "I already sold the others. You're fortunate to get the last one." She rang up the amount. "It'll be three hundred dollars plus tax," she said with a smile.

It took a moment for Conrad to recover from the surprise.

While waiting for the payment the shop owner deposited the pup in a padded basket and handed the entire bundle to Conrad.

Finally Conrad gave her his credit card.

"Three hundred and forty-five dollars for six inches of dog!" he muttered aloud as he walked back to his car. Isabel better be happy with it!

With one hand on the steering wheel and the other delicately holding onto the pup, Conrad drove home. As he entered the house, Isabel came to greet him.

"This puppy has no mother," he said curtly. "He needs somebody to take care of him. Petting, cuddling, that sort of thing...do you think you and Junior can help?" He waved the basket in front of her.

Excited, Isabel grabbed the basket and went to sit in the rocking chair with the pup in her lap. She stroked the little thing, compensated by a lot of licking. "He's cute." She looked at her father and smiled. "Can I keep him?"

"Well...his owner wants something in return." The frown that appeared on Isabel's normally happy face stopped him. Retarded, yes, but very protective of both the baby and the wolf. She had sensed something was going on. Better play it straight. "You know I don't like the dog you had in the mountains," he said, looking sternly into her eyes. "But I like this one." He bent to knead the puppy behind its ears. "Of course, we should give him a name."

"Bobo," Isabel said instantly. "We'll call him Bobo."

Conrad stood in front of her. "Deal then? You keep this pup, the other goes," he said firmly.

For a few moments Isabel kept her lips clamped together; then she mumbled a brief okay, took Bobo with her, and went to the kitchen to fill a dish with milk. The pup drank eagerly, spilling half of the milk on the floor.

Conrad joined his daughter. "Happy?" he asked.

Isabel shook her head, her long hair swaying left and right. "Bobo too small to keep Junior warm."

Conrad kissed Isabel good night. He was definitely too tired to figure out what she meant.

The day after, at lunch break Conrad put his feet on the desk, and turned his thoughts to Isabel and Junior. They had settled nicely, and his home, bustling again, made him feel like old times.

He couldn't avoid, however, wondering what kind of life Isabel had lived for the last sixteen months.

The police had found a man's clothes and boots together with a workbench and several tools. Chopped wood, neatly piled against the back of the log house, was ready for the cold season. Clearly, Isabel had been living with a man. Did he take her to the hospital to have her baby? Conrad took a detailed map of the region and drew a circle around Barnist, the closest village where the log house, built on crown land, was located. He called the two hospitals in the area. As the search drew a blank, Conrad enlarged the circle to include more towns and villages. He repeated the search. Finally he got some results: a hospital one hundred miles from Calgary had a record of a baby born in late August. A teenager who answered to the name Isabel Honey had given birth only half an hour after being admitted. The following day, after having nursed the baby, she had taken off with the child. She disappeared as mysteriously as she appeared.

Conrad asked the hospital staff to fax him the record. As he sensed hesitation on the other side of the phone line, he used the weight of his office. "The baby's data are a key factor in a critical case we're investigating," he said gravely. "It's crucial we get those data as soon as possible."

Two hours later Junior's birth record was in his possession.

With his eyes closed and dressed in the white-and-blue-striped hospital outfit, Junior looked small and frail. *Not to worry*, Conrad told himself. The doctor had found him in excellent shape. Isabel's man must have provided well, concluded Conrad.

But who was the man, and where was he now? Would he go back to the log house? What would he do when he found out that both mother and child had taken off? Obviously there were no simple answers. The truth was Conrad did not have high hopes of tracking him down.

Holding Bobo with one arm, Isabel greeted Conrad with a big hug.

She went to sit in the rocking chair and deposited the pup at her feet. Bobo happily pulled on her socks as Isabel circled her feet all around him.

Conrad knelt beside her. "Isabel, do you know who the baby's father is?" Since Isabel did not clue in, Conrad explained: "You lived with a man. Who was that man?" Isabel did not reply. "Did you cook meals, wash clothes for him?"

After Isabel nodded, Conrad asked, "For a long time?" Isabel shrugged. Concepts of time and distance were difficult for her to grasp. "Did you go walking or swimming with him?"

Isabel's face became radiant. "Yes," she said.

She had some good times with him. Good for her. "Do you have a photo, a picture of him?" Isabel shook her head. "What was his name?"

"Honey, he told me to call him Honey."

Honey! That was no name! The man was probably on the run, Conrad thought in a flash. What better partner than a demented girl? Nobody would believe what she might have to say. "Did he have a car?" Isabel nodded. No use to ask what kind, Isabel wouldn't distinguish a van from a pickup. "Did you meet him at the summer camp?"

Isabel raised her eyebrows and seemed to make an effort to remember, then smiled at Conrad. "Don't know," she said.

The baby, awakening, uttered a few sounds. Isabel promptly rose, picked up Junior and began walking back and forth.

No use trying to talk to her now, since she wouldn't listen, intent only on the child's needs. Conrad sighed. That child was the entire world to her, the first thing that ever entirely belonged to her, and yet, she was not fit to raise him.

It was going to be a big problem, he thought as he flattened in his chair.

It was the third pair of shoes Bobo had been chewing on. "No!" Conrad shouted, as he rescued his leather slippers. The pup waggled his tail, sat in front of him and emitted a noise that was an attempt at barking. Conrad gave him a quick pet. The baby and the dog were running the household, he thought. No harm done, though, since it was a happy place, full of life.

Tonight he would try to find out where Isabel had gotten the young wolf she had with her in the log house. "Isabel," he called.

"This dog looks very much like the one you had in the cabin. Where did you find that dog?"

"In a hole," she said, and blushed.

"With others?" Conrad asked. Isabel avoided looking at him. "It's okay, sweetheart," said Conrad. "There were other puppies?" Isabel nodded. Oh my God, she went into a wolf's den! "How many?" Isabel ticked one, then two. "Weren't you afraid?"

This time Isabel laughed. "Yes, but I waited until the mother was away. I sneaked up and took one pup with me."

Conrad caressed her face. "My dear child," he said tenderly. She had stolen a pup from a wolf pack…but why in the world would she walk into the woods to get one?

8

Stretched out in an easy chair with his arms tucked under his head, Kurt Todd thought about business. He had started as a policeman and learned how law enforcement operated. A few paybacks had helped him accumulate a small fortune, but nothing compared to the success he had enjoyed as soon as he had started on his own. He had looked for small-time crooks, people on the loose without a trade and uncertain what to do with their lives. He had created a tight ring of criminals he knew how to control.

He mentally reviewed the essential traits of his key employees.

Al Garnett's specialty was theft: big or small. With the complicity of his father, who had been serving as a butler in different mansions around the world, Garnett had regularly gathered information on valuables left temporarily unguarded or insufficiently protected. The jewelry and collectors' items stolen by Garnett had produced a vast amount of money for his organization. Stamps had been easy to steal but had not generated a great deal of revenue. Garnett was on the run. To keep him out of circulation, Todd had relegated him in a mountain cottage built on crown land, near Barnist. He had used that cottage himself many times while trekking in the Rockies.

Fred Kusteroff was his trusted courier and messenger. Fred's house was just outside his hideout. He could contact him any time of day or night. He was also his smokescreen. Fred could go anywhere with his cab, talk to people in a casual way, and gather important information without raising suspicion. He lived frugally with his wife and two kids and was very dependable.

Norman Arbib was the weak link in his organization. He had presence and a natural flair, and could sweet-talk anybody. He loved to read and though he had not finished grade five, he managed to use difficult words appropriately; he could easily pass for a college graduate. Unfortunately he often did not follow orders, and that had been the main reason why he had lost on the Gronchi Rosa operation. There was not a great deal of money involved but he, Kurt Todd, should not be thwarted by one of his own. He couldn't lose face in front of his men. That was the reason he had forced Norman to continue the hunt for the rare stamp.

Ron Donavan was one of his most knowledgeable men. His expertise in explosives and electronics had been instrumental in carrying out profitable thefts in small financial institutions not yet protected by sophisticated surveillance equipment. An ex-policeman, Donavan was the owner of an isolated farm on the shores of Lake Erie. The farm itself generated little income, but his barn and shack had been excellent places to conceal stolen goods and weapons.

Clara Moffatt was by far Kurt's best acquisition. She was a good organizer, was the best lover he had ever met, and had no scruples. She could use people and throw them to the lions without blinking an eye. She had made ten tapes that had raked in about five million dollars. The concept of never entertaining a live conversation with each other when an operation was on the go had been the central and most important element of their modus operandi. It prevented them saying things on the spur of the moment—things that could give away somebody's identity or location. While on a mission, Clara Moffatt was instructed never to answer the phone directly and never to call him. She had to leave a message for him on her own machine, making sure to communicate what was important without revealing any compromising details. On his side, Todd would contact her regularly using a phone untraceable to him.

Yes, his girlfriend Clara had performed above expectations. Together, they might be able to successfully conclude the Taillard affair.

Using a stolen cellular he punched in Clara's number and listened to her most recent message. She had wonderful news, she said. She had a promotion; she was now Mr. Taillard's personal secretary. She would work at his residence instead of at the head office of Bergeron & Taillard. Pretty soon she would accompany him on a business trip abroad.

Todd listened to the message twice. It was a fairly standard message: the mention of a trip meant that Clara was very close to concluding her mission and making the compromising tape. Clara's voice had the usual sexy undertone. As Todd heard it for the second time, he began missing her, and wished he could see her and touch her, even if only for a short time. *Was it too risky or could he find a way to approach her unnoticed?*

The shrill of the phone interrupted Todd's thoughts. It was Al Garnett. Todd listened for a few seconds. "What? You are here? Are you crazy?" Todd barked into the mouthpiece. Garnett was supposed to stay in hiding. The police were looking for him for his role in one of the blackmailing operations. "Okay, okay. I'll send the elevator down."

Moments later a big man was standing in front of him.

"You didn't see the big news, eh?" Garnett took off his sheepskin coat and threw it on the floor. "Shit! Am I tired! I walked up and down one cliff after the other to reach this dammed hole. I know this place like the back of my hand, yet it was hell to find in the dark." He looked around to find a chair to sit on. There weren't any. He slumped onto the floor, exhausted.

Todd turned the light to shine on Garnett's face. "You'd better have a good excuse for coming here instead of following my orders."

"What? Oh, I thought you expected me to show up. I see you don't know yet. While searching for the Simpsons' plane, they found Isabel Tormez."

Even if Al Garnett had answered all the questions, justified everything he had done, it was not good enough. Kurt Todd looked at the burly giant, asleep on the floor like an animal. Garnett was an imbecile. If he weren't afraid that the police cut a deal at his expense, he would turn him in. He sighed. He had to find a temporary shelter for the man. But first, he needed to get more information on what had happened in Barnist.

He went to look into his surveillance camera. A dark blue cab was parked at the rear of the cottage. Fred Kusteroff was home and Todd summoned him.

Soon after a short young man with a red mane of hair stood in front of him.

"For the next couple of weeks you're in charge of the Taillard operation," Todd said to Fred. "You know what to do. If Clara needs you, she'll call you. As usual, no personal contact. Keep an eye on her from a distance. Your job as a cab driver couldn't be a better cover." He patted the man on his shoulder. "Now, go downtown and buy me all the newspapers you can find. I need them, right now."

Fred nodded and left as quietly as he had entered.

Todd waited for Fred's return, nervously looking into the camera that continually scanned the area between his hideout and Fred's house.

Fred returned, parked his car and dashed toward the concealed door. Todd sprang it open and brusquely took all the papers away from him. Without a word he dismissed him. He sat and nervously unfolded the *Toronto Star*. On the second page was a huge picture of Conrad Tormez as he was reunited with Isabel and her baby. The next newspaper indulged in a mushy story about Isabel, how her retardation had caused pain and sorrow to her parents, how desperate was her father when the girl had disappeared.

Todd furiously shredded the newspapers. Conrad Tormez surely managed to attract some attention! Now, he would be asked to write the woeful story of Isabel's abduction...and could make a pile of money on it!

Disgusting.

He kicked Al Garnett awake. The man stank. "You've slept long enough. Go shower and get some clean clothes from my closet. I'm sending you back to the Rockies."

"I don't want to go there. It's winter. So much snow...some days you can't move, even with a four-wheel drive. And now, I don't have my girl anymore." Garnett's eyes widened, full of anxiety. "I'd rather go to jail," he muttered.

Todd stroked his temples, knowing that a headache was on the way. This was dangerous territory; if Al went to jail he would sing like a canary. He had no choice but to help Al out. "You'll go to my new house, then. It's barely finished, but there's a generator and the furnace has just been installed. I'll ask Ron Donavan to finish off all the other hookups. We'll get you a sleeping bag and some food." Not even six aspirin would clear his headache. He gave Garnett a cold, distant look. "If you move from there without my permission, I'll have you killed."

He did not have to elaborate. Al should know that he would.

"I hate that mother…." Al Garnett started as he entered Kusteroff's cab.

"You know the boss doesn't want bad language!" Fred Kusteroff cut in.

"Yeah, I know. He's a pimp and wants to play high-class! He thinks he's God. 'Do this.' 'Do that.' 'Move, you're an idiot!' " Garnett lowered the seat back and stretched his legs as much as he could. "Have you seen his new machine, the one he keeps hidden in the wall? He says it's only a computer, but I don't believe him. He'll be able to strike a few keys and turn on the heat in his house—the one in the hills, more than hundred miles away. He's the devil, I tell you."

"Kurt's smart, very smart. He knows the technology needed to be in business. He's a good organizer. He plans every operation carefully. He knows how to get money out of people."

"But not with the last two operations. He lost a bundle, I heard—not from him, of course."

"Shut up. Fifteen months ago we picked you up two minutes before the police came to arrest you. And it was your fault, dropping your driver's license while delivering a blackmail message."

"Okay…." Garnett lowered the baseball cap over his eyes. "But I think there's something spooky about the man."

"Nothing spooky. Kurt explained everything to me. He's gotten a satellite phone—fancy stuff. With that you can call anybody anywhere around the world. He calls his computer in the hills; then the computer switches on and off some of his equipment. That's all."

"Hmm…I'll be in his house, with explosives and all kinds of weapons in the basement. Shit! Once the wiring is finished, he'll turn on the lights, the radio, and other stuff when he pleases. It's scary, it's freaky, I tell you." Garnett shifted in his seat. "And I miss my girl. Before the baby was born she did everything I asked her." He paused and sighed. "After, she wasn't the same. Too busy running after the kid. But even so, it was nice to have her around."

45

9

Ron Donavan

Ron Donavan slowly backed his truck into the shack. Neatly arranged along the walls were bags of fertilizers, seeds, and weed killers; at the back, different-sized barrels stood close to each other. Donavan unloaded the tools and materials he had used to blow a short tunnel on Todd's property—the only non-criminal job he had done in the last five years. He took a black booklet out of his pocket and began updating his inventory. He prided himself on being able to build a custom-order bomb on short notice. He knew his business; he knew how CSIS and FBI analyzed the smallest fragments of a bomb and spent endless time constructing the profile of its maker to determine the so-called *signature*. To keep the authorities guessing at his signature, Donavan made sure to vary the components every time he built a new bomb, and structure each of them in a unique way.

He looked at the stock hidden in the barrels. The sulfuric acid, the nitric acid, the nitroglycerin and the RDX and Semtex explosives were all there in good quantity. Carefully packaged in a plastic container were detonators, hobby fuse, and wires of various sizes. A metal box contained the nails he had carefully made by filing down wire, and a dozen tiny screws from which he had eliminated the tool marks. Everything was in order, he noted with satisfaction.

A member of the Montreal Police bomb squad for eight years, Donavan had retired from the force five years ago and come to southwestern Ontario to live what he thought would be a quiet, relaxing life. He had bought a small farm high on the shore of Lake Erie, and jumped into his new venture with the enthusiasm characteristic of a novice.

One day he was looking at the combine working his 100-acre farm when a car crossed the field and stopped near him. A man got out and introduced himself as Kurt Todd. For a while they talked about the dry season just past and the poor bean crop that would hardly provide a return for the seeds, not to mention the cost of fertilizers and transportation. Ron could use some empathy—he would lose more money this year than in all previous years. He shouldn't have left his job with the police department in Montreal. The pay wasn't great, but it provided him with a fixed income he could count on, rain or shine. Now he was in financial trouble. Not only was his farm heavily mortgaged, but he was also in debt personally.

As Donavan expressed his worries and elaborated on his problems, the man listened attentively, making sympathetic noises. He inquired about his barn, whether Ron had animals, and what he was using his shack for. No, Donavan replied, he had no animals and the barn was used only to house farming equipment. Todd had asked about fertilizers, and whether he had occasion, as a member of the bomb squad, to become familiar with their use in creating bombs.

It was then that Donavan took another look at Todd. The man was tall, with blue eyes that never stopped scouting around, focusing on the corn still in the field, on the barn, and back on the field. The conversation had been, for the most part, superficial, but now Donavan tried to assess Todd's interest in stopping by. "Why do you want to know about explosives?" he asked, suspicious.

Todd shrugged. "Curiosity," he replied, his voice carrying an uncommitted tone. "The corn won't bring in much either, right?"

"Nothing. I won't even bother getting it off. A friend of mine will come and get it to feed his pigs. He'll probably hand me a couple hundred dollars." He tried to capture Todd's attention. "Would you be interested in buying this place? It's high on the lakeshore, so there are no problems with the erosion that's been plaguing most of the shoreline. One day this piece of land will be valuable and profitable when exploited commercially, putting up buildings, for instance."

Todd waved off his remarks. "Too far away from any big cities, as it stands now. Maybe in a hundred years a developer could set up some cottages." He shook his head to reinforce his words. "But surely not now."

It was a dull day in October. Fog was mounting from the lake; clouds, low and gray, were swollen with rain; seagulls swooped down the fields in search of food. A southeastern wind gave foreboding of a storm. "I'll be going," Todd said, zipping up his windbreaker. "If you want a job with me, leave a message on my machine." From his coat pocket he lifted a piece of paper and scribbled a number on it. "I could use both your barn and your shack, maybe even your services." He paused and grinned. "And I'm sure that you could use some cash."

He had gone to work for Kurt Todd. *Unfortunately,* Ron Donavan thought as his mind came back to present time. He had given Todd accurate information concerning the most recent police procedures; shared his knowledge about the most common microcircuits used to create detonators, and actually blown up a few old safes for him.

His criminal activities had provided him with a good income. Recently, however, Todd had become impulsive, more dictatorial every day, hardly accepting even a small suggestion on any operation, and Donavan wondered how long people around him could function effectively. He was growing every day more impatient, almost anxious, to leave Todd's criminal ring.

PART 2

10

It was her kid brother's fault, ruminated Savina Thompson. She got a bubble gum out of her purse and began chewing it with fury. She wouldn't have to even consider Conrad's proposal to impersonate the Woman in Black if she had not told him she would do anything for him if he ever needed help. And that time was now. She would have to behave like another person every time people were around, and take risks for him.

Conrad, of course, was aware of her brief yet intense infatuations for handsome men—that was probably the reason he had dragged Denis Taillard to the meeting when he had asked her to play Clara Moffatt. What Conrad did not know, however, was that after the sad end of her last romance, she had resolved to stay away from men. They were nothing but trouble.

Savina sighed. Life was full of miseries. She blew her gum until the bubble burst.

Denis' image, however, popped up again, unbidden. He had been cordial and concerned; there was no way she could deny he had made an impression on her. The situation was getting dangerous. She should think of somebody who looked like him but had an unpleasant personality. That would help her associate Denis Taillard with negative thoughts.

She reviewed the men she had met in her life. Finally she got the comparison she was looking for. Denis' physical aspect reminded her of her drama teacher: the august Mr. Vincent Major. Mr. Major was the child of two English actors; he had walked on stage at the age of three; he had learned to read and write at the age of five…yada, yada. He prided himself on being a monster of culture—something nobody had ever been able to verify, since he continually talked about himself. But that was not the worst. Every time she rehearsed a scene, Mr. Major stood only five feet away from her and interrupted at least once every minute, interjecting all sorts of remarks: she did not articulate clearly; her tone of voice was inconsistent with the content; her gestures were not smooth...whether she recited Shakespeare or Simon. At best he addressed her with condescension.

She had to come to hate Mr. Major, and finally dropped out of his classes. Yes, Denis' light brown hair, speckled with gray, and his elegant physique reminded her of Mr. Major. She should keep that in mind.

She glanced at her wristwatch. Time to leave for her new job. She shot a nostalgic look at her comfortable sneakers as she slipped on a pair of Ferragamo shoes. She appraised her image in the hallway's full-length mirror. The wool pantsuit enhanced her slim figure and the lace collar of her black blouse added a soft touch to her face. She swung her head left and right, admiring the way her hair swayed. She definitely had a sophisticated look.

She grabbed her purse and left for Denis Taillard's residence.

As instructed, Savina parked her car at the rear of the house, and walked to the front. The chimes had not finished their song when the door opened.

Denis welcomed her into the house and led her into his den. A ten-foot-wide window offered a view of the backyard. Amidst the shrubbery, on the left, two bird feeders attracted sparrows in great number; a gazebo, on the right, housed a barbecue range and two piles of plastic chairs. The den interior was elegantly furnished. A collection of Norman Rockwell plates loomed against the dark paneling of one wall, while bookshelves lined another.

"Nice place you have, Denis."

"Glad you like it, Savina. It's going to be *your*—I mean *our*— office."

"Call me Clara. I have to get accustomed to my new name, or I won't turn around when people address me."

"Okay, okay. You look nice, Clara."

"Do I really look like Clara?"

"Yes, you do. But there was something about her that never convinced me. Every time she walked into my office, she was all smiles and kindness. Too much for real. So I watched her carefully. When she thought nobody was looking, her expression was harsh."

"Oh, that corresponds to the life she was living."

"I guess so. It must be hard to be a criminal, always watching over your shoulder, not knowing who to trust." He paused. "But let's get back to us: let me know how I can make your day pleasant, Savina."

"Clara!" Savina laughed. "Since I'm here as your personal secretary, tell me what you want me to do."

"Do you really want to work?"

"For sure. You pay my salary…so I'd like to make myself useful."

Denis hesitated. "Well, you're trained as a guard…so I should ask you to guard my books. They're mostly booklets related to musicals or operas."

Savina glanced at the bookshelves. "They don't look in danger," she said. "I'm sure I can keep an eye on them while I'm doing something else." She sat on the desk Denis had arranged for her. "I can type. I can use the computer." She shrugged off her coat and hung it on the chair back, waiting for orders.

Denis stood there, clearly embarrassed. "Let's start tomorrow. Today I'd like to show you around. There are some nice trails looping around my property. Covered with some leaves and a bit of snow at the moment, but a pleasant walk just the same." He handed Savina her coat. "If you'd like to be useful, why don't you take some food for the geese? If we feed them they'll stick around all winter long."

Walking side by side, they followed a narrow path and arrived at a pond. They sat on a stone bench, tossing bread chunks and spreading crumbs around them.

"Savina," Denis called, "I'd like you to know that I'm happy I had the occasion to meet you. I enjoy being with you. More than I've imagined."

Savina didn't respond. She enjoyed Denis' company too. The situation could take an unwanted twist.

It was already dark when Savina sat in her Corvette ready to head home. The motor spluttered a few times and died, but not before filling the interior with gasoline fumes. One of the custodians came to help but, after half an hour of checking, he concluded that the car had to be towed to a garage.

Denis came to see what the problem was. "Unfortunately I cannot take you home," he said. "Very shortly I have to go to an important meeting. We'll call for a cab. Tomorrow morning my chauffeur will pick you up."

Within five minutes a dark blue taxi with silver stripes stopped before the gate of Denis' residence.

Savina had just buckled up when a police car, all lights and siren, signaled them to pull over.

"Step out, please, Ma'am," one officer told Savina while the other said to the taxi driver, "License, please." He checked it carefully and said, "Your vehicle isn't registered for public transportation any more. You'll have to come with us." And, turning toward Savina, he said, "I'm sorry, Ma'am, you'll have to wait for another cab."

"In the middle of nowhere? Can you not call me one?"

"We don't do that."

"But I have no way to make a call."

The officer hesitated. "I'll make an exception, because it's quite late."

The cruiser was ready to leave, when another taxi, orange with a green top, pulled up. Conrad was in the back seat. "The driver of the cab you took before, Fred Kusteroff, hung around your place yesterday. This morning he followed you here. His cab was parked along Mr. Taillard's property all afternoon."

"Oh, things are getting hot. My car didn't start. Do you think he might have tampered with it?"

"Possible. But don't get too excited. Kusteroff looks more like an independent operator than somebody who belongs to organized crime. We have already checked him out. It was easy, since his cab's license plate was legitimate. Only expired. And not by much—two months only."

"It's getting scary, Conrad."

"Okay, it could have been a way to keep in contact with Clara Moffatt. I'll know if we trace the cab that Denis called for you. In any case I'll have a chat with Kusteroff. We may get some information out of him." Seated in a corner of the cab, Savina didn't utter a word. "How are things going?"

"Fine. Mr. Taillard doesn't have much work for me. He asked me to reorganize his books, records, CDs, DVDs, and videocassettes."

"I see you're getting settled. We're almost there, so I'll duck while you get out. Keep up the good work, Savina."

11

At the Varlee Country Club Denis was engaged in a singles tennis match. He expected Savina to show up any time. It was only in the middle of the second set that she made her appearance.

Wearing high-heeled shoes, black slacks, and a turtleneck top, Savina made a grand entrance. She sat near his sister, Veronica. It was impossible not to spot Veronica, Denis had told her. Veronica was tall and blond with green eyes. Veronica wouldn't miss coming to the club to watch him play. As Denis changed court sides, he noticed with apprehension that his uncle, Gilbert Bergeron, had come too and was going to sit next to Veronica. Gilbert was his mother's brother and a bachelor by conviction. A good soul, but incredibly nosy. And Denis wanted this encounter with Savina, camouflaged as Clara, to go off without a glitch.

He shot a few balls into the net to bring the game to a quick conclusion.

He hurried up to the tribune reserved for the spectators. "Hello, Veronica. Hi, uncle Gilbert." He bent to kiss his sister on the cheek. Feigning surprise, he turned toward Savina and said, "I didn't know you were a member of this club."

"I'm just a guest, at the moment. I got an invitation to join, so I came to look around. Nice club: tennis, badminton, two swimming pools, a fancy restaurant. And I still didn't visit the pro shop."

Denis introduced her as his personal secretary, Clara Moffatt. "It's a nice surprise to see you here," he said. "Care to join us for a bite to eat?"

"With pleasure," Savina replied, and rose.

Around the table everything was going smoothly, when Gilbert Bergeron suddenly asked, "Miss Moffatt, Clara, I mean, have we met before?"

"It's an old trick," Denis said promptly.

"No, it's for real. I met you. I don't forget a face."

"I did a couple of fashion shows: casual clothes. I don't suppose you were there?"

"No."

"Maybe you met her at the charity dance last Saturday," Veronica said.

Gilbert insisted. "No, it was at a shop. Did you work as a salesperson recently?"

"No." Savina quickly glanced at Gilbert and then at Denis. She needed a way out. She had to think of something convincing enough to stop Gilbert from commenting any further on her or her looks. She winked at him. "I'll let you in into my little secret. I saw the outfit I'm wearing on a saleswoman working at Garments for Pleasure. It's a fancy shop on Queens Quay. It looked great on her. I rushed to buy one exactly the same for myself. Maybe that's the connection."

"That's it! I shopped there two weeks ago."

After everybody left Denis offered to take Savina home. They were just in the limo, when Denis asked, "Did you really meet uncle Gilbert?"

"Yes, exactly two weeks ago. He asked me where the men's department was. We chatted a little. He wanted me to help him choose a tie. I told him I was on duty. He could have my attention only if he stole one."

"You patched it up pretty well."

Savina laughed nervously. "I'm not sure it's permanent. I mentioned the store. That wasn't too smart, but I needed a way out. I felt as though I was going through an X-ray. He may come back with more details next time."

"Don't worry. Next Saturday we play together, right? I'll ask Mother to keep uncle Gilbert busy. He likes to go shopping with her."

On the way to Clara's apartment nobody spoke until almost in town. "I'd like to come up to your place," Denis said suddenly.

"What for?"

"I'd like to give a look at the lingerie you couldn't show off when Conrad was around."

Savina hesitated, then said, "Fine."

The limousine stopped to let the passengers off, then faded away.

As she entered her apartment, Savina glanced at the recording machine: there were no messages. She took off her coat and invited Denis to sit. "Close your eyes while I prepare the show," she said softly.

She came back a few minutes later and lit the floor lamp near the desk. She took Denis' hand and led him to the table. "Now open your eyes," she ordered. Five pieces of lingerie were neatly displayed on the desk.

Denis looked at her, at the lingerie, and back at her. "You're a big tease, you know that?"

"Lingerie you said. Lingerie it is." She held her chin up, waiting for his reaction.

There was silence for a moment. "I thought we could get acquainted a bit…." Denis looked at her and deposited a soft kiss on her neck.

Without looking at him, Savina said, "I don't think it's a good idea to get romantically involved."

"Well, I don't see why not…it'd be nice to create a warm atmosphere for when we'll make the tape." Savina didn't answer and avoided looking at him. "What about a little kiss?" Denis asked.

She neared him and hastily brushed his lips with hers. "Done," she said.

"It's my turn, now." Denis pulled her close, caressed her hair, then pressed his lips on hers. He gave her a long kiss.

Savina abruptly disengaged herself. "No, Denis, no." She reached for the phone and gave him the receiver. "Call for your limo, please."

Men! They were all the same. They could turn on the charm on any occasion and with any pretext, and expect a woman to fall for it. Could Denis really think that a couple of smiles and dining at a fancy club would do it? She slumped on her bed, totally dressed. She missed her daily routine: patrolling Garments for Pleasure; looking at the dazzling new items just arrived; talking to an occasional customer; going out with the crowd for a late supper or a show; and jogging with her best friend, Theresa Albrecht…. She sighed. Her life had been turned upside down—and all in the matter of a couple of days.

What's next?

She stretched her arm toward the night table and took Clara Moffatt's daily planner, which Conrad had photocopied for her. Savina looked at the next couple of occasions Clara had listed to casually meet with Mr. Taillard. There was a good one, she noted with pleasure. On Wednesday they would go see *The Lion King* at the Orpheum Theater; Saturday they would play tennis. She didn't care for the game, but at least she would not have to wear black, since the club dress code was strictly white.

She rose and took a shower. As the warm water splashed over her body, her thoughts went back to Denis. She had to admit that he had managed to clear out the unpleasant comparison with her old drama teacher. Denis was much younger to start with, vitality sprung from his well-built body, and his boyish smile was definitely captivating.

She should stay on her guard. After a hard start, her life had taken the right turn. She had a job she liked and paid reasonably well. She had a hobby she greatly enjoyed, and she had a few very good friends. She shouldn't do anything foolish that could change all that.

Even Conrad had recommended she be careful. Under his laid-back appearance, he had told her, Denis Taillard was a strong-willed man who spared no effort to reach his goals.

12

Who said strenuous physical exercise was invigorating? Forty minutes of running after a tennis ball left Savina out of breath and all sweaty. She asked Denis if they could cut it short and quickly headed for the showers. When she began combing her hair she realized that her natural waves popped up all over, more vital than ever. Damn! Out of her big sports bag she dug a bottle of hair spray and drowned her hair with it. She kept combing from top to bottom, one stoke after the other. She wondered whether she could ever pull it off as the Woman in Black. Denis' uncle, Albert, had almost recognized her, and she hadn't spent more than ten minutes with him. And that problem with the taxi driver who had stalked her for a full afternoon? And then Denis: he took their encounters as pretexts to court her!

After twenty minutes her hair finally resembled Clara's. She marched out of the Ladies' room and, ignoring Denis who was standing by, neared the exit of the club.

Denis ran after her and took her sports bag off her shoulder. "My chauffeur will carry your bag to the car."

"Why?"

"My dates don't carry any luggage."

Savina stopped and stood in front of Denis. "Why? Are they crippled?"

There was an embarrassing silence for a moment, then Denis commented, "You can cut people pretty hard, you know...."

Denis gave Savina's bag to the driver and slid into the car to sit beside her. For a moment there were no spoken words.

Savina's troubled heart took the best of her. She turned her head away from Denis to hide her tears. "Sorry...I didn't mean to be nasty," she mumbled. "You've been very kind. It's just that...that I can't be one of your girls. I don't walk, talk or move like any of them. Look at the hands: mine—they scrubbed floors; theirs—I bet they never touched a cleaning product!" She sobbed. "And I'm not sure I can be Clara." She pulled on her hair. "Look here. My hair has not been stretched properly. My curls keep popping up. I can't go to a hair saloon either—and believe me, the agent at the police station who has worked on my hair doesn't know much about hairdressing."

Denis tapped on her hand. "That's okay, Savina. Everything is going to be okay. *I* am the one at fault. I should have kept my mouth shut."

* * *

A big mural, showcasing a shoreline immersed in azure waters with a black-and-white church looming against a hilly background, welcomed the patrons of the Amalfi Restaurant. On the left a gigantic rack held wine bottles, each lying flat and tagged with make and year. From the ceiling over the bar, on the right, glasses of every size hung upside down. At the back of the vast room three arches led to small rooms for private gatherings.

In one of these Conrad was waiting for Denis, wondering why his friend had called a meeting.

As soon as he walked in, Denis sat at the table and opened up to him. "I feel we should call the entire operation off. Savina is very uneasy about playing the part. In a crowd she feels inadequate, and with me she's paranoid about getting close."

"Meaning what?" Conrad asked bluntly.

"She's very conscious of the fact that she doesn't look like any of the girls in my league."

"Of course she is. I am, too, and so are you." Thank God, this was a minor issue. No reason to be alarmed. "The fact that she doesn't dress or behave like the women in your social environment is the best part of all. The struggle to fit and fake is evident. Her skin isn't soft enough to be a successful blond and a touch too dark to wear black. Clara's was even darker! No girl would do anything of the sort except if she had a purpose. Clara had it, and Savina fits Clara's appearance. She's a perfect impostor, a faithful imitation of Clara. That's the key issue!" Conrad called for service. "What's next? You didn't ask me here just for that, right?"

Denis nodded. "That was the main reason." Quietly they placed their orders. "Any progress on the entire operation?" he asked.

"Clara Moffatt has received one call from her so-called employer. The most difficult part was explaining the extra two-day absence, when Clara, directed to visit her mother in a nursing home, had the fatal crash. We've explained the unexpected delay convincingly, we believe. Since Clara's mother passed away that very same day, we talked about the necessary funeral arrangements." Conrad couldn't avoid showing his satisfaction. "Our speech transposer, Pappa-pappa, is performing wonders."

He continued. "A phone number resulted from this first part of the operation. It's a new lead, pointing to an import/export company with no capital and only one part-time employee. We're pursuing that."

"What about that cab driver?"

"Nothing definite, I'm afraid."

Denis seemed much more at ease now. "You don't have to spend this coming weekend with Savina," Conrad said. "Take some time off. I'll invent something to be sure that she isn't called in to report to her mysterious employer. Okay?"

"No, I like the girl, I really do, it's just that...sometimes her defenses are so high that I don't know what to think or say. I believe she detests me."

Conrad gave Denis a permeating look, as if to prod his mind. He said, "I wouldn't think that.... Next meeting in three days, unless something unusual happens."

The next day Savina was friendlier, though still quite reserved. Denis had convinced her to watch with him *La Traviata*, a registration of an opera made at the season's grand opening of La Scala. Savina had been restless during the entire show, shifting from one position to another. Denis retrieved the DVD from the player and stored it in its case. "Worried?" he asked.

"Yes, very worried. I expected my employer—whoever he is—to leave instructions for me or at least ask how the operation was going. Instead, nothing. Not a single message in the last three days. Conrad finds it strange, too." She rose and reached for her purse.

"Going already?"

RENE NATAN

"Time to quit. I made a list of your opera and ballet books and watched a beautiful show." She laughed. "We can call all that hard work!"

"I'm happy you love music, and opera in particular. We can go to a big show, when this operation is over." Denis rose too. "Do you have any engagements tonight?"

"Savina is out of circulation, but Clara is available."

"What about preparing supper together?"

"Sure. I'm happy to be useful. And being active, for me, is the best way to relax."

"We divide the work. I'll set the table, open the wine and light the candles."

"That's heavy work! What do I do?"

"You invent the meal. It wouldn't be safe in my hands."

"That's probably the best way to share the preparations." Savina moved into the kitchen, full of energy.

In the middle of the table a small vase held a nosegay of forget-me-nots, whose color nicely complemented the pale blue decorations on the Rosenthal china dishes. The soft light of six blue candles gave the room a warm ambiance. Denis admired his work, then joined Savina in the kitchen. "Everything smells so wonderful. I'm famished." He helped Savina serve a vichyssoise.

Denis complimented the soup, then asked, "What's next?"

"Stir-fried chicken with vegetables. It's one of my favorite dishes." She walked back to the kitchen and returned with a heated chafing dish. "Here it is. Let me scoop some for you."

They were savoring their meal, when Savina asked, "Are you sure they don't know you're separated from your wife?"

"Pretty sure. The divorce was finalized a week ago. Conrad asked us to keep it quiet. Nobody knows, except the interested parties, my family, and our lawyers." Denis winked at Savina. "I'm totally available." As Savina didn't respond, he said, "Tell me something about yourself. Ever married?"

"No. I'm not yet ready for family life. It requires commitment." She paused to sip her glass of Cabernet Sauvignon. "I like my freedom: playing in amateur theater when a part becomes available; staying out at night as long as I please, that sort of thing."

Denis lifted his glass and said, "To you, Savina. That all your dreams may come true."

62

13

Savina returned to her condo late, pleased about the time she had spent in Denis' company. He had been friendly and attentive, and she had discovered something they had in common: the love of music.

She was fumbling for the light switch, when a hand grabbed her shoulder, making her entire body freeze instantly.

"Hi, babe." A man was breathing on her neck. "Long time no touch."

"Oh…hi." Who was this man, and what did he want from her? How did he enter her apartment without being seen? A chill went up and down her spine as he pulled her close to him.

"I thought I could do without you for a while…but I can't. I want you," the man whispered in her ear. He took Savina by the arm and dragged her toward the bedroom.

A gun rubbed against her body. Oh my God, he was armed! That meant trouble. She could be trapped.

"What's the problem?" the man said and gave her a shake. "You're still my girl…Kurt's girl, right?"

Savina summoned all the courage she had. "Of course," she said evenly. "I was just surprised to find you here."

* * *

In the condo where the stakeout was taking place, detective Dean Perkins contacted Conrad. "Somebody is in Savina's place. She returned ten minutes ago and there is no light yet. I captured noises in the hallway. Footsteps—a man's footsteps, I mean. Now, I can hear whispering."

"Did you see anybody entering the house?"

"No. Nobody got through the main door. He must have entered through the balcony, at the back of the apartment. I can't think of any other way."

"We can't do any checking without blowing the entire operation. On the other hand, if somebody is in Savina's apartment, he has time to harm her. We have to think of something."

There was a moment of tense silence on both sides of the telephone line.

"What if I call the fire department and start a fire right away?" suggested Perkins. "I have tons of newspapers besides me and I'm heavy smoker. The setup is plausible."

"Fine. Do it. I'm on my way."

* * *

"You sound strange...." the man said.

Savina could hear the rustling of clothes: Kurt was undressing himself. She strained her eyes to perceive a few features of the man who called himself Kurt. She couldn't, since only specks of light filtered from the outside. "I've been suffering from an allergy. It affects my throat."

"You even talk different!" Kurt said, sounding suspicious.

She had to respond. On the spot. "But I bet I fuck the same."

"That's my girl!" Kurt pulled her close and pushed her onto the bed.

"Compound number 45: total evacuation. Right now." The message broadcast loud and clear.

"It's this one!" said Savina, trying to hide the relief in her voice.

Kurt jumped to his feet, walked over to the closest window, lifted the sheers and peered out.

"What in the world...a fire truck and two police cars!" With two big steps he reached over to the other window and looked out. "Shit! The condo next door is on fire! It may be dangerous. Let's have a quickie."

A new message resounded in the air. Savina immediately recognized Conrad's voice.

"Condominiums numbers 45A, 45B, 45C: we are coming to assist you to evacuate. Get a housecoat and be ready."

"I have to flee," Kurt said, and grabbed his clothes.

"Can you?"

"Of course, I'm wearing a police uniform. I won't have any problem getting through."

A couple of minutes later two officers entered Savina's place, followed by Conrad. All the lights were suddenly switched on. "Any damage?" Conrad's piercing eyes scrutinized her.

"No. But it was scary...for a moment he noticed I sounded different!"

"We'll get him, he can't be too far, and everything will be over."

"I'm afraid not." Savina explained then said, "The only clues I gathered are that he's tall, his name is Kurt, and he was Clara's man."

"Damn!" Conrad rushed outside shouting orders while Savina sat on the bed, shivering. He was soon back and shook his head in disappointment. "Vanished," he said. He sat close to Savina and lightly stroked her back. "Let me think. Today is Tuesday. I'll ask Mr. Taillard to leave earlier for the trip. I'll call him right now."

"It's *very* late."

"It's *very fine*, believe me." Conrad stayed on the phone only a few seconds. "Pack all your stuff," he said. "One of our taxi-look-alike cars will take you to Denis' house right away. He's expecting you. You'll stay with him. Don't come back here. It isn't safe. We'll use the speech transposer to brief your employers about what you'll be doing directly from our station. I'll let you know what we've told them tomorrow morning. Call me around eleven."

Conrad was calm, in spite of the emergency procedures he was inventing on the spot. He patted Savina on her shoulders. "Going to a friend's place to spend the night, after what happened, is a logical action. So there's nothing to worry about."

Denis was waiting on the entrance steps. He silently took Savina into his arms. "I have a warm tisane ready for you. Come." He helped her with her bag and took her to a bedroom on the second floor.

"No need to tell you how sorry I am for the problems we're causing you. I'll never be able to make up for any of them."

"It's over now." Savina sat on the bed and sipped her herbal tea slowly. "I'd like to lie down, Denis. I'm exhausted."

Denis nodded. "Have a good rest. My bedroom is next to yours. I leave the door open. Call me if you need anything."

65

14

At four o'clock in the morning Conrad dragged his feet into a dark house. He kicked off his shoes and turned on the light near the door. Quietly he entered the family room. Isabel had fallen asleep in an armchair, Junior sprawled against her chest. *What a beautiful sight!* For a few moments Conrad stood there, mesmerized. Then he retraced his steps, went to the kitchen and poured himself a glass of orange juice.

He felt totally exhausted. It had been some night—but no harm had come to Savina.

Operation Woman in Black was getting hot, yet he had no leads. Alone in his office the following morning, Conrad pondered the situation, nervously drumming his fingers on the metal desk. He did not like the recent developments. The few phone messages received by Savina had produced no results since each incoming call had come from a public or a stolen phone. Worst of all recently a click at the beginning of the communications revealed that Clara's messages were being taped. Why? The last thing Conrad wanted to see was a permanent record of Savina's disguised speech.

And Fred Kusteroff? Nothing of substance. He had justified his stationing close to the Taillard's and Moffatt's residences with calls from customers who had not shown up. Believable, if not true. He had paid the fine without blinking an eye and renewed his license right away. Frustrating, Conrad concluded. It was necessary to forget about the schedule found in Clara Moffatt's planner and shorten the times. Make the tape, deliver it, and free Savina.

Last night's encounter had been a close call—he didn't want any others.

He should meet with Savina and Denis and propose a new course of action. He called Denis and asked him to take Savina to the country club. After the events of the previous night, playing tennis would relax both of them. He would arrange for the club to reserve a private room for a meeting later in the afternoon. But now he had to report to his boss. He should prepare for the meeting carefully, since his boss had never been too enthusiastic about Operation Woman in Black.

The Varlee Country Club, a two-story building in natural stone, stood in the middle of a big hollow. On the right, well sheltered by the prevailing wind, were eight clay tennis courts; on the left, covered with a shiny tarp, lay an Olympic-size pool. Indoor tennis and badminton courts were housed under inflatable domes. A colonnade surrounded the main floor of the clubhouse; cast-iron tables and chairs lined up neatly under the arcade. Even in mid-winter guests could sit in the open yet protected area to sip a drink or have a snack. The club belonged to the Bergeron & Taillard Company, which used it as a convenient outlet for its sporting goods.

Conrad parked his car and headed for the clubhouse. He felt silly in white shorts and T-shirt in the middle of November, but he wanted to shed some of his professional look. Swinging his racket up and down, he reached the room he had earlier reserved for the meeting with Denis and Savina.

Dressed in black, with her hair still wet from a recent shower, Savina looked like a frightened kid — much younger than her twenty-six years. Denis was seated close to her, a worried look on his face.

"Nice of you to have ordered coffee and snacks. I had no supper last night and forgot about breakfast this morning." He grabbed a quichette while assessing their moods. His boss had left him no choice. The operation could go on only if Savina felt like continuing. He needed to spread a feeling of calm, even of normality, if possible. "I've thought about the situation. If Savina still agrees to be part of the operation, we shouldn't lose any time. Clara Moffatt mentioned a resort area in Jamaica — it's in her planner. I suggest you both leave right away and make the tape." He sipped the coffee Denis had poured for him.

"It's risky," Denis said. "It was risky since the beginning. It appears they have an eye on Savina, Clara that is, even when they seem to have no contact whatsoever."

Conrad ignored him. "Savina? It's your decision. We choose a different place for your vacation, to be sure they don't have any connection to where you and Denis go. I think we can justify that. There is never a live conversation between Clara and her boss, so that makes things easy. You leave a message, as usual. Now...Denis' family has a cottage in the British Virgin Islands—a beautiful place, by the way." He zeroed in on Denis' face to assess his reaction.

"That's a great idea! They'd have no time to organize anything over there." Denis turned to face Savina. "It's near the ocean with a little private beach. You'll love it."

"Settled then." Things were going smoother than he expected. Denis had agreed. He was the person whose approval was critical. He knew Savina would follow. "The only consequence is...they may not believe in the tape you're going to make. It'll be their choice, but my instinct tells me they'll make use of it."

Savina looked straight into Conrad's eyes. "I like the idea of getting it over and done with it."

Conrad grabbed a handful of nuts and rose from his seat. "Great," he said. "I'll look after the details and get you copies of the tapes Clara has made to get you familiar with what needs to be done."

15

Garments for Pleasure was an expensive shop on Queens Quay, with big windows decorated in exquisite taste. Theresa Albrecht had waited months before being assigned to the women's department, the most elegant and lucrative division of the store, but finally she had made it.

Theresa looked at the scarves hanging on the rack and changed their order. They were so beautiful that it was difficult to decide which to display. She did not expect any more customers; with a storm warning in effect, she thought, most people would head home instead of indulging in shopping.

Then an old car rolled into the deserted parking lot.

Holding the collar of his sports coat, a young man entered and quickly shook the snow off his hair. He began browsing, stopping here and there to check the price tags. He approached the counter where Theresa was standing and smiled at her. "Maybe you could help me," he said.

"Certainly." Theresa had just finished a course for salespersons. 'Never let a customer walk out without buying,' had been the last words of her instructor. "A purse or a scarf?" she asked.

"I don't know. It's a gift for my mother. For her birthday. Something simple...."

He has no money, Theresa reasoned. No use trying to sell him a purse, since they were all of the finest leather or suede. "We have beautiful scarves—big and square or long and narrow, whatever your pleasure." She unfolded two on the countertop. One was red with blue arabesques, the other was bright green with stripes of gold.

The man fingered them both, then said, "I can't spend much. Not more than twenty-five dollars." He smiled, showing his even teeth.

He had come to the wrong shop. The scarves started at forty dollars. "That may be a bit of a problem." She should tell him sorry and let him go. But he was buying a gift for his mother. *How moving.*

The man was staring at her. "Have we met before?" he asked. "My name is Norman Arbib."

She shook her head no. Surely she would have remembered such a hunk. "Theresa Albrecht," she said. "The shop will close soon and tomorrow we have a twenty-four-hour promotional sale. There is something I can do for you, Mr. Arbib."

"Norman," he corrected her.

Theresa reached under the counter to get at a big box. "They're going to tag these half price." She pushed aside the expensive scarves and lined up half a dozen others. "These will come to about twenty-five dollars, tax included," she said. "Which do you prefer?"

"You choose," said Norman.

"Your mother has blue eyes and dark hair, as yourself?"

"Yes."

"She'll love this one," Theresa said as she unfolded the delicate pale blue fabric in front of him. "Very popular. It's called 'Waves of the Ocean.'" She turned around as she heard somebody approaching.

A man in uniform walked up to them. "Time to close up," he announced. "It's nine."

"Be done in a minute," Theresa replied. She quickly wrapped the scarf and slid it into a gift bag.

The guard tapped his fingers on the counter. "Any details about the mysterious trip Savina won?" he asked Theresa.

"Not a word." Theresa rang up the bill and gave the receipt to Norman. "I don't even know how she did it! A trip around the world! She had no time to explain, she told me. She was in a big, *big* rush!"

"Some people are simply lucky," the guard said and headed to check the alarm system located near the main entrance.

Norman had not moved. "Is there any place around here I could grab a coffee and a doughnut, or something like that?"

"Oh yes. The Wiener Konditorei is just around the corner. I always stop there for a late snack. They make the best Sacher Torte in the country." The man was poor, but handsome. She might end up buying him a snack. "I can take you there. Just wait for me outside, then follow my Camaro."

Norman's old Chevrolet would not start. How embarrassing. He kept turning the key while shooting worried looks at Theresa. Thank God, she was busy sweeping the snow off her car.

It had taken him months of painful searching to latch onto Theresa Albrecht. For a long time she seemed to have disappeared from the globe. She was the only link that could help him recover the precious stamp known as the Gronchi Rosa.

His mind began to play scenes of the past. He would never forget when he first entered the Friends of Austria Club.

The club was located in Scarborough, a suburb of Greater Toronto. It consisted of only one large room whose walls were full of posters. Opposite the entrance was a desk; behind the desk sat a young woman, Marg, dressed in a Tyrolese costume: white top, red and green skirt. Norman approached her and mentioned the annual party that had taken place at the Victoria Hall. He had only glanced at the crowd that night, he said, but he still had the occasion to briefly talk to a nice girl.

Norman was only halfway about the description of the woman, when Marg exclaimed, "Disappeared!" She shook her head. "I can't understand why. For the last two years Theresa saved money for the big trip the Club was organizing. She didn't talk about anything else. We don't know what happened to her." She gave a quick look at Norman. "Maybe we should go to the police. Together, I mean."

Norman responded with a grin. Theresa Albrecht! It was in her pocket he had dropped the stamp! He had seen her only from the side. But once he had mentioned that the girl was tall with a prominent nose and thick glasses, Marg had quickly come up with her name. "It won't be necessary, Marg. I was just in town and thought of saying hello. Many times she mentioned this wonderful Club." He glanced at the posters behind her desk: one showcased a huge church; another, a boat gliding on still waters; a third, steep rocks and snowy peaks. "Maybe you can tell me something about the trips you organize."

"Sure," the woman said. "Take a seat."

"Thank you, Marg." Norman desperately needed more information. "Theresa is a kind girl," he ventured, hoping to get Marg going.

"She surely is. Always ready to help others. A good soul. Took care of a difficult mother—I never heard her complain once." Marg rose. "Let me show you some of our most popular vacations."

She picked up a few pamphlets from a high shelf and unfolded them in front of him. "This is the trip which interested Theresa so much. Three weeks on the Danube, starting in Krems, ending in Breslau, with a five-day stay in Vienna. Fairly inexpensive, since the group would travel on a freight boat."

Norman wondered where the girl had gone while Marg pointed at another flyer. "This is a trip to the Tauern Berge—very exciting if you like climbing, trekking, and rafting." She paused, seemingly puzzled. She turned around and pointed to a poster hanging on the wall. "That is our most exclusive tour: Salzburg, for the Mozart Festival." She smiled at Norman, in an attempt to draw his attention. "I bet you like good music."

Where had the woman gone? Did she sell the stamp? God, he would never find her. She would not be on any of these cheap trips. She would be sailing off the coast of California on a luxury cruise. "Thank you," Norman said. "I'd like to become a member of this wonderful club and learn a bit more about your tours."

He gave her a smile. One of his last ones, if he couldn't recover the stamp.

A jagged noise called him back to reality. His engine had started. Relieved, Norman nosed his car in behind Theresa's Camaro. Minutes later they reached the Wiener Konditorei.

Theresa sat at a corner table and gestured Norman to sit in front of her. They were about to open their menus when the owner invited Theresa to the kitchen.

Through the kitchen's glass partition, Norman watched Theresa. Was she the woman he had been looking for? Theresa was gorgeous, with beautiful red hair and fine facial features. Nothing of her resembled the unattractive girl he had seen at the Victoria Hall more than a year ago.

He should find out more about her before spilling the beans to Kurt Todd. It would be a pity to disfigure her—and Todd would not hesitate to do it, even if he only *suspected* that the girl had anything to do with the stamp. Even worse, he could order him to do what had to be done in order to recover the Gronchi Rosa or the money it was worth. And he, Norman Arbib, hated violence. If Theresa had indeed found the stamp, maybe he could convince her to return it.

"Are you all right?" Calling from behind, Theresa broke his reverie.

"Yes. Just hungry." He forced a smile. "But let's talk about you. Tell me something about yourself."

16

Big snowflakes covered Theresa's windshield before the wipers had time to clear them. She should not have stayed at the Wiener Konditorei so long. But Norman had been very pleasant company. Handsome and with a melodic voice, he had made her feel like she was the center of attention all night long. She had told him of her invalid and domineering mother, the many times she had tried to find a reasonable relationship with her, her own incapacity to break loose until her mother died. She had told him of the excitement of working at a fancy shop in town, her friendship with one of the shop guards, and the many miles they jogged together.

Something was strange, though. Norman had said very little about himself. Theresa shrugged. No big deal, really, since they had a date for next Saturday. At that time she would have an occasion to ask him about his job—if had one—and whether or not he was married. Her life was at last going in the right direction. For nothing in the world would she start a relationship with somebody who was not available or did not have a solid job.

Norman wanted to charm the girl, make her talk about The Friends of Austria. He sprayed himself with the last few drops of aftershave and got dressed.

With a bottle of wine in his hand, he knocked at Theresa's door. As he entered her apartment, a smell of baking hit his nostrils. "Smells delicious," he said with sincere appreciation.

"Hello, Norman," Theresa said as he gave her the bottle of Merlot. "Thank you."

"Sorry I'm a bit late." It had taken him almost an hour to convince Fred Kusteroff to lend him the ten for the wine.

"It's okay," she said cheerfully. "We'll skip the snacks and sit right away at the table. Why don't you open the wine?"

"Sure." Norman sniffed the air. "What are you cooking?" He was hungry, very hungry.

"A special dish of veal, fried apples, bananas, and pineapple, with rice. But what you smell is a strudel, my grandmother's recipe."

"German?"

"Austrian. That's where my family comes from." She smiled ruefully.

"And yourself? From around here?" Norman asked casually as he poured the wine and offered her a glass.

Theresa did not answer and quietly sipped on her wine. "The food is ready: Hawaii Schnitzel, one of my favorites."

The dish was fabulous. He had not eaten in two days, and savoring the food seemed to be more important than playing investigator. The girl was a great cook, in addition to being a stunning beauty. He lifted his face to look at her and asked, "Can I have more?"

Theresa nodded and scooped another portion onto his plate. "I'll get the dessert ready. Whipped cream on top?"

"Sure. I hope you don't feel neglected," Norman said. "I just wanted to compliment your cooking. It was the best meal of my entire life," he added.

"Glad you liked it." Theresa came back with the dessert and looked intently at him. "Tell me something about your job."

What could he tell her? He had been demoted from the rank of gangster, even if of second category, to that of casual worker in a hotel. His last job consisted of spreading manure on the lawn. While working he was supposed to place cameras to film who was coming and going. "I'm the outdoor manager of The Hermitage Resort Complex," he finally mumbled.

Theresa's eyes opened wide. "You work at The Hermitage? The one east of town, on Road 16?"

"Yes. Do you know it?"

"Of course! It's a beautiful building, set in a fantastic location, with a lot of shrubs and flowers in the good season. It's part of my jogging tour. I loop around it twice, when the weather permits."

"Alone?" Norman asked.

"Until a few weeks ago with my friend, Savina, the guard who won the trip around the world. You heard of her, right?"

Norman nodded. "I don't mind jogging, but I prefer cross-country skiing in the winter. It's more fun," Norman said. "There are beautiful trails just outside town."

"I never did any cross-country, but I'd like to try."

"We can go together. There's enough snow already. Any day?"

"Tuesday? It's my day off. I'll have time to get some equipment." Theresa hesitated. Then, "Would you come with me?"

The woman was playing beautifully into his hands. "Of course. I know of a shop in town with good skis and even better prices. I'll pick you up early in the morning, say nine o'clock?"

"Great." Theresa poured coffee into two china cups. "Norman, I hope you don't mind if I ask you a personal question. Are you married?"

Married? Norman laughed. How could he ever think of getting married, when he was constantly sent all over the country, to deliver stamps or to communicate orders, for scant compensation? And no insurance for all the things that could—and would—go wrong? "No," he answered. "I never found the right girl." His eyes bore into hers. "Not until now."

Theresa threw her head back and laughed.

She was definitely very sexy, wrapped in that green dress that looked like a second skin. Too bad he couldn't trust her.

Cross-country skiing had been fun. Theresa was a good sport, she laughed when she fell, she tried hard to follow his instructions and she had responded to his kiss without hesitation. *Too soon to check up on her?* Maybe so, but Kurt Todd had not given him much time.

Even if he didn't know whether he was welcome, Norman rang the bell of Theresa's apartment. He carried a large pizza. Theresa looked in the pinhole and opened the door. "I thought you might be hungry but too tired to fix dinner."

Clearly surprised, for a moment Theresa didn't move; she just knotted tight the belt of her white terrycloth robe.

"Here I am at your rescue. You lie down and I'll serve you a couple slices of pizza."

"Not a bad idea. I am not that tired, but my face feels tight and cold, and my legs and arms hurt. But I really like cross-country skiing." Theresa went to stretch on the chesterfield.

Norman sat on the floor close to her and opened the box. "I can make coffee, if you like."

"No. There's beer in the fridge," said Theresa. "Better than coffee, when you're thirsty."

"Great. I'll get it."

Two bottles of beer had their effect: Theresa lay placidly on the sofa, asleep. Norman adjusted two pillows under her head, and covered her with an afghan.

He slowly finished his beer and all of the pizza. He began wandering the premises. All furnished in white, the bedroom had two single beds; the doors of the built-in closet were two huge mirrors that made the room look double its size. The bathroom furnishings were lilac and matching guest towels lay on the vanity top; the kitchen was small, all in black and white. The only other room in the apartment served as dining and living room; the TV set and the CD player stood in one corner; a table with four chairs was in the middle; the sofa where Theresa was lying and an antique desk lay along the other walls.

That last piece of furniture was definitely of interest. Norman circumspectly opened the first drawer. It was full of stationery, wrapping paper, gift bags, and ribbons. The second drawer contained bills, neatly arranged by year. He would examine them later. But in the third drawer he found what he sought: flyers from the Austrian Club, Theresa's membership card, the CAA tourist guide for Austria, and a large map of Europe. So Theresa was the woman he was looking for. He reopened the second drawer and looked at the bills and bank statements. He found doctors' reports on surgical interventions.

He sat on the chair beside the desk and leafed through the papers. *Interesting reading*, he thought. He shot a glance at Theresa, as she changed position to lay flat on her stomach. She was thirty-eight years old. She did not look her age.

As he put away the reports, Norman's hands felt a large, sturdy envelope. He grabbed it. It contained letters, all in German, from the same person. The sender was Herr Werner Schröder, Advocat, Leopoldstrasse 42, Krems, A5209, Õsterreich. That correspondence could be important. He would borrow it, photocopy it, and have it translated. Norman softly closed the drawer. He picked up the afghan that had slipped onto the floor and arranged it again over Theresa.

Satisfied with his findings, Norman left Theresa's apartment.

* * *

All her life Theresa Albrecht admired one thing above all: beauty. She admired it in flowers, in paintings, and in women and men alike. She never felt envious of others, though, convinced that only some were born to be on top with looks and success, whereas all others had to lie in their shadows.

Things were different, now. Thanks to the inheritance from her late aunt, she had been able to afford cosmetic surgery. Her cheekbones and nose had been reshaped, laser surgery had eliminated the need for glasses, and teeth implants had given her a dazzling smile. Men turned their heads when she walked by.

The more days that passed, the stronger she felt that going to Austria, even if only for a short while, was a must. Two days of blizzard had damaged the big windows on the first floor of Garments for Pleasure; the department store had to close for urgent repairs— a full two weeks. It was an excellent occasion to fly to Austria. She could finally see if her late aunt had been given the dignified sepulture she amply deserved.

Tears raked her cheeks every time she thought of that glorious day when she had received a big cushion mailer with a brief note and myriad loose stamps. The note said:

> *Meine liebste Nichte!*
>
> *Ich kann Dir wenig überlassen, mit Ausnahme von diesen Briefmarken. Diese können etwas Wert sein. Auf jeden Fall hoffe ich dass sie Dir Glück bringen.*
>
> *Deine Dich liebende*
> *Tante Maria Theresia*

Did they ever bring her luck! She had added to them the few stamps in her possession and contacted the Austrian lawyer in charge of her late aunt's affairs. More than a year had passed since. Her life had changed radically, and definitely for the better. Yes, it was imperative she go see where her aunt lived and died, and put some flowers on her grave.

PART 3

17

Toward the Virgin Islands

Savina lay in bed, meditating on the upcoming trip to the Caribbean. Naturally her thoughts went back to Denis. A nice fellow, Conrad was right about that. But he was a man…. Her experience with men had been dreadful. Her last boyfriend viewed her as a reflection of himself and, every time the reflection did not fit the original, he would get upset with her. And the boyfriend before him…he was a yuppie from City Hall, who belittled her for being a policeman manqué and constantly criticized the way she dressed.

Maybe Denis was not that kind of person. Maybe…but to be on the safe side she should keep her defenses up. She should get a grip on reality: they did not belong together, their social environments were miles apart, they had only a few habits in common, and they perceived the world from different angles—she weighed her actions in terms of money and consequences. Denis was totally void of anxiety. In his life everything had fallen into place, and he obviously trusted that it always would. He seemed ready to make love to her, apparently unconcerned about the feelings he might arouse. She should watch out since their time together was just a brief digression.

She had a job to do, and she should do it well, and with that resolution, Savina finally fell asleep.

Late the next morning they were in the air. Denis, who had replaced the pilot after takeoff, was flying the plane that would take them to their tropical paradise.

Reading was not successful—Savina was unable to concentrate on one single page. She closed her book and stared at the ocean, fascinated by its immensity.

Finally the plane started its descent. Landing would be left to the professional pilot, she had been told. In fact soon after Denis came to sit close to her. He wore a soft gray sports shirt and matching trousers, and an ivory belt whose clasp carried the ensign of the Taillard family. His thick blond hair, coupled with his tanned skin, made Denis a very attractive man. He rubbed her arm to get her attention. "Today you look particularly beautiful, Savina," he said.

Savina laughed. "I must, considering the price of my clothes!"

"I didn't compliment your clothes, Savina, just *you*." He hugged her around the shoulders. "Just give me a chance to make these days pleasant for you."

Her arm linked with Denis', Savina was absorbed in the unusual tropical sights: palm trees were outlined in sharp profile against the clear sunset; a sandy beach stretched a full mile; and a cutter anchored in the bay swayed gently in the water. As they walked amid the thick foliage, a low structure suddenly made its appearance.

Denis invited her into the bungalow and gave her a tour. "I hope you'll like it here. It's where my family normally spends a few weeks to escape the coldest months. My sister Veronica decorated this bungalow using creamy colors, except for the kitchen, which is bright orange."

"Everything looks beautiful. I've never seen anything like it, except on TV," Savina said.

Denis patted her shoulder. "Let's freshen up, and meet for supper."

Once in the guest room, Savina quickly dug out of her suitcase a pair of linen slacks and a black tank. She changed, opened the patio door, and descended barefoot the few steps leading to the private beach. Boulders and small rocks amassed left and right, grading into the ocean to protect the small bay from the high waves. Savina went to meet the water, splashing her feet and watching the imprints she left on the wet sand. She walked back and forth then sat on one of the rocks.

Everything around her seemed to be out of a luxury vacation catalogue. The place belonged to dreamland…. How was it possible for some people to be so wealthy? Of course she knew the Bergeron family was old money and so were the Taillards — they had settled in

Quebec two centuries before and moved to Varlee only forty years ago. But still…Savina couldn't resist a smile as the image of the little house she grew up in drifted in her mind. It was a small ranch with a cottage roof and metal sidings. A protective roof sheltered the only car they owned. It was a happy place, though. Her mother was always busy in and out of the house, and her father spent every free moment playing with his kids. After her father had tutored her in the difficult art of target shooting, the teenaged Savina thought she was ready to take on the world, no obstacle insurmountable and no task too difficult. It was strange how that view had changed the instant her parents had died, shot by an assassin with no name and no face.

Until a few weeks before, even if she was aware of the existence of wealthy people, she had never thought of being part of their world, propelled into a beautiful environment, all of her needs being taken care of. Once again, life had taken a strange turn. What weeks ago appeared to be an absurd operation she had been coaxed to be part of, seemed now to be a wonderful occasion for experiencing something new and exciting. Even if only for a short time, she intended to enjoy every second.

The sound of a man's steps overcame the soothing murmur of the waves. Denis was standing behind her. "The custodian brought in our dinner: prawns, calamari, and scallops, marinated in one of the local zesty sauces and grilled to perfection." He extended his arm to help Savina rise.

"I got lost looking at this fabulous place," she said. She took the hand Denis offered her and together they walked back to the bungalow.

They sat around the veranda table ready to savor the seafood. The custodian poured a delicate Chablis into long-stemmed glasses and placed them alongside the white place mats trimmed with deep purple pansies. Black ironstone dishes, centered on each mat, enhanced the elegance of the table. For a while, Savina and Denis exchanged more looks than words. It was dark when fruit and coffee were served.

Savina nibbled on a wedge of a fried banana, then speared a slice of pineapple, sucking the fruit off her fork. She was definitely enjoying the meal. The ambience had a taste of magic, and she hoped the evening could last forever.

"How do you feel, Savina?" Denis asked.

"Relaxed and impressed. This place is fantastic." She looked up. "The sky, tonight, is so clear one can count the stars."

"Glad you like it." He tossed the napkin aside, put his elbows on the table, and cupped his face with his hands. "I'd like to know how you feel about me—if it isn't too much to ask." Savina kept her eyes down, then glanced left and right. "Too hard of a question?" Savina shook her head. "So, let me in."

Finally Savina met his eyes. "I like you too much for my liking," she said in a soft tone.

Denis threw his head back and laughed. "What kind of statement is that?"

"You're a wealthy man...."

"I was born that way. No fault of mine."

"We don't belong together." Her voice was not more than a whisper.

"We won't know until we get together."

Savina did not reply right away. Then, "I'm afraid of getting hurt. There, I've said it all."

"I don't mean to harm you in any way." Denis winked. "I can supply you with good references concerning my behavior."

It was Savina's turn to laugh. "I'm sure you can. Too many, probably."

Denis spelled out his words. "I said good, not many!" He reached for her hand. "Just tell me, Savina. Is there a little place in your heart for me?"

Oh my, he was tempting her.... Savina took some time before replying, "If I did, what would you do with it?"

"I'd sneak in and try to get it all. I can't stand competition in love affairs. Absolutely none."

"Ah, it is so...." Avoiding getting romantically involved was going to be more and more difficult. The man was swathing her with attention. He was dammed good looking and even his voice was suave.

"So, do you have that little corner available for me?" Denis asked again.

"I do, Denis," she mumbled. At this point nothing seemed more natural than surrender.

"Oh, that's great news!" He rose and extended his arm toward Savina. "Come, come with me, sweetheart. I have a surprise for you."

In the guest bedroom a gigantic bouquet of flowers towered over the ivory-colored bedspread. "I chose the tuberoses for their perfume and the flowers of paradise as my heartfelt wish for you, Savina," Denis said. He stood there, waiting for her reaction.

Savina bent to sniff at the flowers. "They smell wonderful. Thank you, Denis."

"Do I deserve a kiss?"

Savina neared him and pecked him on the cheek.

"Is that all?"

She turned her face away then gave him a sidelong glance.

Denis put his hands on her shoulders and asked her, "Savina, do you still have reservations?" His hazel eyes brimmed with desire. "You know I want you, don't you? I got a look at your body: a beautiful body that holds only a few secrets from me. And I love your eyes, so full of life, and a touch of mischief." In a flash Denis' mouth pressed on top of hers as he hugged her tight.

When he let go, Savina said, "You know what Conrad's order is? Not to get emotionally involved with you!"

"Conrad, Conrad! The man is a thousand miles away," Denis said with annoyance. "Forget about him!" He unbuttoned her top and bent to kiss her neck. "I want my woman to be involved. I love when she responds to me." He unhooked her bra and put his arms around her naked back. "And, unless your eyes lie, you will."

He slipped off her top, and blindly tossed it into a corner. He unzipped her slacks and slid them down slowly as he caressed her bare legs. Then, "You're cold, and your face is white. Something's wrong?"

Savina stood in front of him. Not a muscle moved in her. Was she making the same mistake, thrusting a man, all over again?

Suddenly Denis pushed her away from him, keeping her at arms' length. He scrutinized her face. "Have you ever been hurt by a man?"

Savina hesitated, then she replied, "Not physically, no. But most of my boyfriends hurt my feelings." She looked straight into Denis' eyes. "Not most, all of them."

Denis gently caressed her hair. "I won't do that to you, Savina. Actually, I don't think I have never done that to anybody—not on purpose or not without a very good reason." He paused. "I want to gain the trust of people around me. And once I have it, I won't betray it."

"Those are nice things you said." She leaned against his chest and hugged him tight. When she let go of him, she looked at him with a twinkle in her eyes. "Is that the reason you were undressing me?"

"Not really. I had something else in mind, and you'll soon know what it is." He pressed his mouth to hers, a light taste at first, then a plundering, his tongue probing and dancing with hers. He streaked up to her buttocks, hooked his fingers in her underwear and let the laced garment fall down her legs.

It was playtime now, Savina thought, and she began to unbutton his sports shirt.

Denis did not wait for her to reach his trousers. He slipped off the belt and unzipped them. With a quick movement he swept the bouquet of flowers out of the way, and pushed Savina onto the bed. He lay beside her, his hands moving over her body. "I wanted to get close to you the first time I saw you," he murmured. "But after you modeled the black wardrobe, I wanted to do a little bit more than get close. I wanted to touch you, taste your mouth, suck on your breasts…." He bent over her, took her nipples in his mouth until they became hard. He spread little kisses all over her neck, slowly reaching for her ears; his teeth began nipping at her earlobes. "I'd like to keep doing this all night long," he murmured.

"But I have a slightly different idea," she whispered in his ear. She couldn't wait. She stretched to reach his briefs and pulled them off, then delicately guided his hardness into her. And then there was nothing else Denis could do but rock within her.

Savina's body followed his rhythm; her eyes opened and closed; her throaty moans became louder and louder; her hands, clinging to his back, tried to pull him closer and closer while her mouth searched for his. Denis was bending over when she bucked once more, and fell back, a cry of pleasure mixed with release filling the room.

"That was quick!" said Denis, and laughed.

"Sorry," Savina murmured. "I couldn't…."

"No problem," Denis replied as he slowly pulled out of her. With his fingers he wiped pearls of perspiration from her face. "No problem whatsoever," he repeated, and smiled at her. "The first period of the show was short, so the second will have to make up for it."

18

The waves rippled into white laces as they eased onto the beach. Stretched on two long chaises and sheltered by the bungalow's awning, Denis and Savina sipped coconut juice from the same fruit.

"I had no time to ask you or Conrad why you're so committed to this operation," Savina said. She raised her chaise to sit straight.

"The director of my company, Marcel Carvey, was also my best friend. We sailed and played tennis together since we were in our twenties." Denis paused. "Marcel had an affair with Clara Moffatt. One single weekend at The Hermitage. That weekend finished his life. He couldn't cope with the humiliation of being exposed since, in spite of everything, he cared very much about his family. He took his own life."

"Sorry to hear that."

"I vowed I'd do everything I could to put away the people who destroyed him. I went to talk to Conrad about it. Marcel was also a friend of Conrad's." Denis lifted himself up to look into Savina's eyes. "That was the reason I listened to his idea, even if it was a crazy one. Now I'm happy I did. I had the occasion to get to know you."

"Thank you. Want more juice?" Savina asked.

"No. You can finish it."

Savina sucked all the juice, making a horrible noise. "What about your wife, what went wrong between the two of you?"

"I guess it wasn't right to start with. We married three years ago after a long relationship. She wanted to travel. Last year, after Marcel died, I took over as director of Bergeron & Taillard. I couldn't leave. That was the most recent difference we had. But, of course, there were others." Denis stopped, pensive. "She kept postponing having a family, for instance, even though she was thirty-four." Denis sighed. "I wasn't really married. I just paid her bills."

"You don't plan on seeing her anymore?"

"Oh no. We kept our divorce quiet, but it's final, believe me. I often asked myself if she was the right companion for me. Now I know she wasn't." Denis rose. "And I'm not the same person I was weeks ago. Marcel's death first, and your presence after, have given me a strong taste of reality. I saw what a non-privileged person has to go through, in life." He extended his arm and caressed Savina's face. "I should tell you how much I admire you for your character. You took care of your brother, and you were so young yourself. You accepted a favor from Conrad; you felt obliged to return it, and, in doing so, you're risking your life."

"You really like me!" Savina said. "At the beginning I thought you felt obliged to…to feign an interest in me."

"No, Savina, I wouldn't do that. You commanded my attention since our first encounter. You had beautiful hair. Soft, wavy but not curly, long…incredibly long. And a golden brown, the best ornament a woman could wear. And you cut it for us. I felt terrible when I saw you with short, tinted hair." He pushed a few tendrils behind her ear. "You have put a lot of effort into the Clara role. I had no idea what Conrad meant when he said that there was only one person who could play that role and that person was you."

"I like to act. I can imitate accents and different gestures to display a variety of feelings. I used to mimic Conrad with his low voice, his Hispanic intonation of some consonants, and his way of looking at people so close he becomes cross-eyed." Savina bent close to Denis' face and made the imitation. She laughed then sighed. "What I didn't grasp was that this kind of acting could last days, not just a couple of hours. At first, it was hard since I was always afraid of making a slip!"

"I remember our first days together. In the presence of a third party you were tense, and you made a sovereign effort to keep me at a distance. I was so puzzled that I talked to Conrad about it. I thought you disliked me." He winked at her. "But last night you cleared my doubts. I hope we can keep seeing each other when this operation is over."

Savina looked at Denis quizzically and sadly, without saying a word. Clearly Conrad had not told him what would happen if the bad guys suspected Clara's substitution.

"There's a minor issue to clear up," Denis said and rose. "You like your man immediate and passionate, you said the first day we met. Is that true?"

Savina laughed softly. "What I said was meant to stop Conrad from spelling out all your good qualities. It was annoying to hear how good you were!"

"I understand. You were entitled to be mad at both of us." He glared at her. "In any case your lover-to-order is here." He pulled her up. "I can be very immediate," he whispered. "And I'm naturally passionate."

For hours the wind had battered the seashore. Denis' cutter, anchored in the small bay, rolled incessantly, its mast rhythmically swaying back and forth. Sheltered in their cozy bungalow, Savina and Denis had spent a full week totally oblivious of the outside world, immersed in the discovery of each other's feelings and thoughts.

After an unexpected and abrupt call from Conrad, however, they realized it was time to work on the famous tape.

"Did you read Conrad's instructions?" Denis asked while putting a camera on the windowsill. He arranged the curtains to hide most of it, leaving only the small lens unobstructed.

"Yes, I did." Savina blinked her eyes, perplexed. "The entire setup looks complicated. I hope I can do it."

"You have the easy part. You just have to lie down."

"Well, I have to take off my robe showing only my back. Then I have to move in the center of the bed while you get in front of the camera, so that my face is covered by your shoulders. I must show Clara's ring while I hug you. Hmm…."

"Don't worry. We'll rehearse a couple of times. Now the camera is in place, and it's reflected into a mirror. That's how our Woman in Black took her pictures. Now let's look after the lights. Clara always had two or three lamps turned on."

"What strange tastes!" commented Savina.

"It turns out that's pretty good for us, Conrad told me. Lights situated in different spots cast shadows in different directions. The presence of all those shadows makes the details less perceivable. So it's easier to confuse the viewer." Denis paused. "And we need to fool our bad guys."

Savina, her blond hair revived by a recent shampooing, sat on the edge of the bed, trying to concentrate.

Denis knelt at her feet. "Still worried?"

"A bit. The idea of making the video sounds funny, now. Much more than before."

"It is," replied Denis, kissing her. "For me too. But we have to do it, now. So let's try. I'll start taping. We can do it over and as many times as necessary."

When Savina let her housecoat drop slowly, Denis moved in front of the camera and went to lie beside her, propping on his right elbow, the upper part of his body screening Savina's.

"I have my briefs on," said Denis suddenly.

"You can take them off now," suggested Savina.

"But we can't talk!" Denis, laughing, fell flat on the bed. "We can whisper, make noise, but no straight talking, remember?" He rose. "Let's start again. I want to be sure I always start at the beginning, just in case we get it right."

Things were proceeding smoothly, when Savina burst into laughter. "You're so funny when you fake it!" She hid her face against the pillow, still laughing.

"That wasn't nice, you know." Denis shook her shoulders. "Not nice at all."

"Sorry, but I couldn't resist. You close one eye...." she said covering one of her own.

"Try to be serious. And don't undermine my job, just because you have the easy part: lying flat on your back." He rolled her toward the edge of the bed and said, "Up, up. Let's start over."

Two hours later they were eating popcorn while watching the latest version of the tape.

"We aren't doing well, you know," said Denis, depressed. "You're an actress. You should advise me."

"Well...maybe we should film the real thing...."

"No way!" Denis said emphatically. "That's ours. Private. Sacred. I don't want my woman on tape while she's making love to me."

"It was just an idea."

"Don't even think about it," said Denis. "Rather, let's try again."

The phone rang. "It's Conrad," Denis said covering the mouthpiece. He listened. "Sure," he said. And then, "Real soon." He listened more, patiently. "She's well. She says hello to you." He listened again. "I'll call you as soon as the tape is done. Goodbye, Conrad," Denis said and rang off.

"He's growing impatient," said Denis "He's afraid they may try to contact you, that they be able to trace where you are. It'd be a disaster, he claims. He's worried."

"I understand," said Savina, pensive. "Conrad may be also worried about other things."

"Like what?" Denis kept busy rewinding the tape.

"He may be concerned about me. About you and me, I mean."

"Oh?" Denis asked, surprised. "And why would that be? Conrad knows well that if a woman doesn't want me I leave her alone."

"That may not be the reason. He may be afraid of the consequences, if you and I are...if we become...if we were to get involved. That's what he might be thinking. We stayed on the island much longer than planned. And the tape isn't done yet. Conrad is accustomed to guessing why people act in a certain way. And he guesses right, most of the time, believe me."

"You have funny ideas. You talk like I'd represent danger to you. Exactly as you did at the beginning. Keeping me at a distance even if you liked me, as if falling in love with me would be a catastrophe."

Savina gazed at him, a veil of sadness on her face. "Sorry Denis," she replied at length. "Sorry you got that impression. Falling in love with you has been wonderful. No matter what might happen to me, I don't want you to have any doubt about it."

"That's better, much better," said Denis. "Now, are you ready for an Oscar-winning performance?"

19

One advantage to traveling at night is the lack of traffic, Conrad Tormez thought as he drove the last mile that separated him from home. He had problems that needed to be addressed. Isabel had refused to go back to school, since she wanted to be with her baby. Day after day Conrad had relied on Bernice Berstow to keep his family going.

In the last few years his friendship with Bernice had become a solid relationship and, even before Isabel's return, Conrad had been waiting for the proper moment to propose to her. Bernice was an excellent homemaker; she helped at the local toy store in the summer, when several employees took their holidays at the same time, and at Christmas time when the shop had to deal with myriad people. She loved cooking and inventing new recipes; she knew of all kinds of handcraft, and regularly made available her creations to the church bazaar. Bernice had relied on him to help her with Jerome, who was an impulsive and at time reckless teenager. Jerome was also easily influenced. In the past, when Conrad talked to him, Jerome went straight for a couple of weeks. But last time, when he wanted to quit high school, Conrad had not been able to dissuade him. After several sermons, Conrad had finally convinced him to enter an apprenticeship. At the end of the program he would be a certified electrician.

Conrad was anxious to play the father's role more consistently, as a way to compensate Bernice for all the help and support she had given him with Isabel.

Yes, I had to talk to Bernice. But first he had to find out all about Isabel's life in the mountains, and that may take some time.

He parked his car and entered the house.

He had just closed the door behind him when Bobo ran toward him, stood on his hind legs and scratched his trousers. "Down!" Conrad shouted. Bobo replaced the scratching with whining. It was time for his walk. "Later," Conrad said and petted the dog.

He tossed his coat onto the rack and walked into the kitchen. "Busy?" he asked Bernice.

Bernice laughed. "Was I ever! So busy I felt twenty years younger, even if my back kept reminding me that I'm over forty. I haven't sat since early in the afternoon. First there was Junior's bath, then the canaries escaped."

"Oh, my poor canaries! I forgot about them the last few days." He turned toward the cage. "Still alive, I see." He gave Bernice a grateful look. "An angel visits my house regularly. Without her, nothing would work."

Bernice smiled at him. Her two brown eyes became very much alive when she looked at Conrad. "Wait until I tell you all that happened today!" She took two dishes out of the microwave and set them on the table together with two glasses of milk. "Finally I sit. Bathing the baby was something to remember. Isabel and I were ready to plunge Junior into the plastic tub, when Bobo put his paws on the rim. We all got wet, except, of course, the baby." She began to eat her spaghetti with meatballs. "Then I decided to give the birdcage a good cleaning, since it needed it badly. The canaries took off, chased by the dog. Isabel wouldn't stop laughing." Bernice paused to drink her milk. "So I sent Isabel and Bobo outside, and got your fishing net out. It took some doing to catch the two little rascals, but I finally did it."

Conrad stroked her arm. "Thank you, Bernice."

"What about you? You came home late the last few nights. Problems?"

"Yesterday we had a big problem at the station. But the reason I'm so late tonight is because I was in contact with companies that sell and install security systems. We need one, and I was looking for a good price."

"You still think Isabel's man may show up?"

Conrad nodded. "Even if he wasn't there when we arrived, the man must have visited Isabel on and off. There was an awful lot of canned food. Wood had been chopped…it was a strange situation. I want to prevent Isabel or the baby from getting hurt, *in any way*." He pushed his empty dish to the middle of the table. "Excellent. The food was really good." He patted her hand. "Thank you for your help. I don't know what I'd do without you."

Bernice clasped his hand into hers. "You know I like to be useful, and I love to putter around your house. Jerome is busy with his apprentice program; he got some wiring to do for one of the garage's customers. So when he came home he was very tired. He went to bed right away."

"Does he like his job?"

"So far so good. This customer will pay him directly for the work he's doing. Jerome was very happy about that."

Bernice rose. "Good night, Conrad. I need a good rest now."

Rudy Ashwald tossed a newspaper onto Conrad's desk. "A follow up on the Simpsons' story," was the headline of the Varlee Dispatch. Mrs. Simpson's body had been found lying hundreds of feet away from the plane with that of a dog, both buried under a thick layer of snow.

Too bad for the Simpsons, but a happy coincidence for me, Conrad thought as he glanced at the paper. It had been during the search for the Simpsons' plane that Isabel's refuge had been discovered. Thanks to that accident Isabel was now home, safe and happy.

"Have you read the details of the plane crash?" Rudy Ashwald asked as he walked by.

"I don't do any reading, except for the headlines."

"The Simpsons' baby boy couldn't be found. The press still wonders. But I don't see why, considering how wild is that part of the world. With wolf dens spread all over, what do you expect? The animals had a good meal out of him."

The words wolf and den rang a bell in Conrad's brain.

That night Conrad waited until Junior was sound asleep before continuing what had become the usual evening interrogation. "Isabel," he started. "After the baby was born, Honey, your man, did he ever come back?"

"Yes. He picked me up when I left the hospital. We went home together."

"What happened then?" Isabel did not reply; tears began raking her face. Conrad knelt close to her and took her hand into his. "What happened to the baby?"

She turned her face away from him.

"Did he get sick? Just tell me." Conrad rose to get some Kleenex and dried her face. "It's important, sweetheart, very important." He crouched beside her.

Finally Isabel murmured, "Asleep. He was always asleep. Wouldn't wake up."

"The baby was dead, right?" Conrad patted her slim hand. "Isabel, remember when we had secrets? Something we kept for ourselves, only for ourselves?" Isabel nodded. "What you tell me will be *our* secret. *The biggest of all*." He paused to avoid distressing her. "Honey buried him close to the house, right? And put a cross on top of the grave?"

Isabel nodded and threw her arms around her father's neck, her chest shaken by relentless sobs.

Now things started to add up. Conrad stroked her back and caressed her hair until she calmed down. "So you heard barking and went to see." Conrad was patiently putting together the pieces of recollection Isabel was offering him. "What did you find?"

"A baby and a dog. The dog was on top of the baby." Isabel paused, her eyes staring into the distance. "The baby's face was cold, the dog was warm."

"What did you do, Isabel?"

Isabel didn't reply right away. Then she said, "I took the baby in my arms. I licked his face. I licked it and licked it until it became warm. I tried to get the dog up. It made noise but it didn't move...it was cold. Then I walked home." Isabel became suddenly alive. "I nursed the baby, changed his clothes, made a big fire. To keep us all warm." A smile lighted up her delicate face. "I went back for the dog. But it didn't want to come."

"It was then you went into a den to get a puppy?"

Isabel hesitated, her eyes unusually alert. "Yes. I thought it was good, to help keep the baby warm."

Conrad pulled Isabel close and hugged her tight. His girl...she had saved the infant's life, but she would never be able to get credit for it.

Outside Bobo whined and scratched the door insistently, clearly wanting to be rescued from the cold weather.

Conrad watched his daughter as she reached for the door. Isabel looked so much like her mother. Her height, her feminine figure, and her long dark hair reminded him of his late wife. But Isabel's eyes were without light; her perception of the world blurred.

He sighed. It was imperative he take action. There were two things he had to do, and one of these was not to his liking.

He should install a security system; put a video camera near the main door to monitor who came to see Isabel. Her man, Honey, whoever he was, might attempt to contact her. Her story had been reported by all the country's news media. The man would have no problem finding where she lived. And then he should take Isabel to a doctor to prevent any further pregnancy. That was the thought that distressed him the most. He knew how much Isabel enjoyed being a mother.

The snow had been falling since early in the morning. Clearing the driveway was the chore on top of Conrad's to-do list. He had been very busy following the installation of the security system and he had nailed bars on all main floor windows himself.

The snow could wait, he decided. He stretched out on the sofa and pondered the problem that Isabel and her baby posed. When does a person become a criminal? Almost everybody commits infractions to the law, from speeding on the road to hiding goods at customs…but those do not make a real criminal. A criminal infringes the law in a much deeper way.

He shut his eyes.

Conrad Junior was not Isabel's baby. Even in the vast confusion of her mind, Isabel was aware of it. And now so was he. If he kept silent, he would be an accomplice to child abduction. And that would make a real criminal out of him.

A soft knock on the door interrupted his thoughts. It was Bernice. She entered the room and stood in front of Conrad without saying a word, creases of worry marking her normally cheerful face.

"What's the problem, darling?" Conrad asked. "Is it Jerome?"

Bernice nodded. "He didn't come home for two nights in a row," she said, and sat on the sofa. "He's up to something." She paused. "It's that fellow with the blue cab. He came to pick him up."

Conrad took Bernice's hand as tears welled in her eyes. "Tomorrow I'll stop by the garage where Jerome works, and see if he's still there during the day. Nothing we can do right now, Bernice. And don't torture yourself. You've done everything you can for your son. We can't live our children's lives. Let's just hope for the best." He caressed her short, gray hair. "Come close, Bernice. Let's watch a movie together."

20

For the third time Kurt Todd listened to Clara Moffatt's last message, recorded the day after the strange fire at her condo had forced him to leave in a hurry. The communication was brief and to the point, as usual. Something had come up, Clara said, and she would leave for the Caribbean a bit earlier than originally planned. The destination was the British Virgin Islands—not to worry, everything was under control.

Todd was pleased. He could relax: Clara knew what she was doing. He rubbed his hands together.

It was time to check on the fantastic house he was building in the hills: once finished, it would provide him with very comfortable living quarters from which he could operate undisturbed. He would then abandon his rocky hideout near Lake Erie, where he had only the essentials.

An hour later he was there. Since he wanted to avoid Al Garnett as long as possible, Todd didn't enter the house right away; instead, he lingered outside.

A 30-foot cliff separated the clearing in front of the house from the remaining farming land; another cliff of solid rock stood opposite the rear of the building. With satisfaction Kurt Todd admired the house front wall, all made of gray stones, and the skylight that broke the monotony of the big black roof.

He turned around and went to check on the tunnel.

The engineer had given him a hard time and asked a ton of questions about that project; the excavation company had charged him an exorbitant amount of money, even if one of his own men, Norman Arbib, had done most of the digging. But the 400-foot tunnel piercing the rock at the back of the house was now complete. Only small amounts of sand and dirt needed to be removed.

Todd climbed the steep stairway at the back of the house and entered his new home. As he walked into the kitchen, he noted that lunch was on the table. *Great.* He had to admit that Al Garnett was a good cook; it was a pity he kept repeating the old song, that he missed his girl, Isabel Tormez.

"How long do I have to be cooped up in this hole?" Al Garnett asked as soon as he saw him.

"Until Clara comes back. We can't afford any false moves right now. After the Taillard affair is concluded, I'll get you new documents and smuggle you out of the country."

Garnett was going to reply when Kurt put up his hand. "End of discussion, Al. You stay here until I give you permission to leave."

* * *

I'm going to be very careful, Al Garnett thought. *So careful that Kurt Todd would never know I left the house.*

With the skidoo he found in Todd's garage, Garnett reached Highway 62 just after dawn. He then hitchhiked up to the outskirts of Toronto, and walked into a Budget rental. Driving an old Honda he arrived in Varlee by midday. He knew very well where the Tormez family lived.

He knocked at the door as a salesman of chocolate bars at the irresistible price of seventy-five cents each. As he rang the bell, the woman at the door said *no,* even before he could show her his merchandise. Detective Tormez was not taking any more chances with his girl, Garnett thought, or at least so Tormez believed.

But tonight things were going to be different. Conrad was retained at the police station by an anonymous call Garnett had made.

On foot Garnett approached Conrad Tormez' house carefully, avoiding making any noise. The house was plunged in semidarkness with only one feeble light in the kitchen and another upstairs. Helping himself through the branches of a maple, Garnett reached the upper floor, walked onto the balcony and peeked inside the bedroom where the light was on.

Isabel was rocking the cradle, and the baby lay placidly on top of a blue sheet.

He softly knocked on the window.

Immediately Isabel rose and came near. She stood still, her arms behind her back.

Garnett tried to lift up the window, but he couldn't. He signaled Isabel to do it. Isabel shook her head. *What an idiot*, Garnett thought. *The girl is totally demented.* He took a tool out of the purse he was carrying around his waist and cut a circle in the window glass with his diamond-tip cutter.

He was reaching for the inside handle when a siren pierced the air. A blast of light shone in front of him, then a second one and a third, blinding him. A hand over his eyes, he quickly withdrew and fumbled for the branch he had used for climbing to the second floor. He tumbled to the ground and ran toward the backyard fence. He stood still for a moment, trying to gain his bearings.

In the background he could hear the wail of a police car approaching. With an ultimate effort he jumped over the dividing fence, crossed the properties of two adjoining houses and headed for his rental.

Conrad punched in the digital code to open his house door. He shouted orders left and right while he rushed upstairs.

Isabel stood in a corner, shaking, the baby in her arms. She immediately gave the crying infant to her father and said, "I can't help him. He doesn't stop crying." Tears flooded her eyes, and she began shaking.

With one arm Conrad grabbed the baby; with the other he hugged Isabel. Her body felt more frail than usual. "It's okay, sweetheart," he said. Conrad stroked the baby softly and tried to let go of Isabel. "Get the soother, sweetheart, it might help Junior."

Isabel didn't move, instead she recoiled into Conrad's arm and set her head against his chest. *I have two babies here, that's my problem.* Conrad looked around, spotted the soother near the crib and gave it to Junior. Holding the baby high on one shoulder he walked into Isabel's bedroom, almost carrying her. He neared the bed and deposited her onto it. "Go to sleep, sweetheart," he said. He kissed her on the check and caressed her hair. "Don't worry. I'll take care of everything. Junior is safe."

Still sobbing, Isabel nodded.

Conrad closed the door and reentered Junior's room. To Rudy Ashwald, who had just walked into the room, he ordered, "Get the pictures in the camera developed at once. I want to see who the intruder was."

"That bastard!" Conrad shouted, and threw one picture after the after onto his desk. The mysterious Honey was one of his old pals, Al Garnett! Conrad banged his fist on the desk. "That bastard!" he hissed again. Garnett knew of Isabel, of course, and of the camp for disabled children where Conrad took Isabel every summer.

The name Garnett brought back memories more than twenty years old. Albert Garnett, Dale Vernon, and he had gone to the police college together, served in the lowest ranks together, and dreamed together. Until one day, during an operation that was meant to capture five of the most dangerous mobsters, Conrad had discovered that Vernon and Garnett were on the take. In the last stage of the stakeout they had tried to corrupt him, then tried to send him home; and when all had failed, they had wrestled him to the ground. Only a shot in his leg had stopped Conrad from fighting, and often that wound flared up and still made him limp. But the pain he felt then and every time he remembered that horrible moment was not only physical: it was the deep hurt of betrayal.

Al Garnett! He was going to get him, if it was the last thing on earth he did, and he would make him pay for the hardship he had caused Conrad and Isabel!

Conrad took the three photos and drove home.

Isabel was helping Bernice bathe the baby. Conrad patiently waited until Junior was all nice and clean then took Isabel into the family room. He showed her the three pictures. "Is this man Honey?" he asked her. Isabel nodded. "Was he here last night?"

Isabel became agitated. "Yes, but I didn't let him in. He might take the baby away. That's what he told me many times when he got angry."

Conrad sighed. The man deserved the worst. And if things were left up to him, Al Garnett would get the absolute worst. "You did well, Isabel. But don't worry. Nobody will take the baby away from you." He caressed her face. "Now, let's go and see if we can make Junior giggle."

103

21

Back in his refuge on the shore of Lake Erie, Kurt Todd thought about his ongoing operations: the Taillard affair, the recovery of the Gronchi Rosa, his precious stamp, and the moving of explosive from Ron Donavan's farm to his house in the hills. He couldn't do much about the first one since he had to wait until Clara's return from the Virgin Islands. He'd better start to work on the second, then proceed to the third one. He sat in front of his new Apple computer, checked his email and went to the Web sites that dealt with stamp collections. On the Bolaffi page he read interesting news that prompted him to summon Norman Arbib.

**

It was seven o'clock in the morning when Todd's peremptory call got Norman out of bed. He hated getting up so early, but Todd did not leave him any choice. He slipped on the worst pair of trousers he had—a discolored pair of jeans with holes on the knees—and a sweater with sleeves that, shrunk in an endless number of washes, rose well above his wrists. Maybe Todd would feel embarrassed by his looks; he surely couldn't hope to arouse his sympathy. Grudgingly, Norman drove to Todd's refuge. He had plenty of reasons to be grumpy. Theresa had left a message for him: Garments for Pleasure had to close for urgent repairs and had asked her to take her holiday at the same time. She had canceled their weekly cross-country skiing and flew to Vienna, from where she intended to visit her late aunt's place. That was pretty strange since she had never mentioned her intention to take any trip.

When he arrived at Todd's hideout, Todd addressed him without preamble. "Any news about our stamp?"

"Nothing definite, I've matched most of the names of the Friends of Austria club with their current addresses. You can't believe how many people move and don't notify anybody. A lot of work." He was not going to tell him what he had learned about Theresa. She was really a nice girl and may not have found any stamp in her pocket.

In spite of Todd's anger, Norman continued, "Two hundred and sixty members, spread all over the country. When I dropped the stamp into one of the members' pocket, it was at their annual meeting. More than two hundred people."

"All female?" Kurt asked sarcastically.

"No...." Kurt had been such a pain; he'd give him the twenty-six thousand dollars out of his own pocket—if he had it. How wonderful it would be to shake loose from Kurt Todd, since the life of a criminal had become pretty tough. In the last two weeks he had made two trips to the Food Bank. He felt woozy, at times. "Can I sit?" he asked.

"No." Kurt kept him under the fire of his fierce eyes. "I called you in because I've traced the recent sale of a Gronchi Rosa: Vienna. Sold for twenty-six thousand dollars by a reputable outfit. Whoever sold it must feel at ease, since everything seems legal." He paused. "You don't know anything about it, of course."

Norman wobbled. He groped for the chair behind him and let himself fall into it. Oh my God, Theresa, with that honest face, was in it.

"Get up," said Kurt as he tossed onto the table a piece of paper and a bundle of bills. "Here is the auctioneer's address in Vienna. We may be not able to recover the money—assuming that the Gronchi Rosa was our stamp—but we can find out who gave it to them, when and how. Get names. That's your new assignment. We can't afford to be outsmarted. It'd be the end of our business." He gave Norman a despising look. "Try not to get robbed in the process. There are thieves out there."

Still shaking, Norman rose. He quickly pocketed money and paper. "Thanks," he managed to say. "I'm on my way."

Eagerly, Norman counted the bills Kurt Todd had given him and made some calculations. A week in Vienna at one hundred dollars a day was not going to be a luxury vacation but it would guarantee him two meals a day and a reasonable accommodation. He booked the flight, packed his carry-on, and left. On his way to Pearson airport he stopped at the Language Experts Office where he had taken Theresa's documents for a quick translation.

The British Airways Boeing 777 had just taken off when Norman began reading the correspondence from Theresa's lawyer in Krems. The Gronchi Rosa had been sent to him together with another twenty-two hundred stamps from different countries. The notary had checked the authenticity of Maria Theresia's letter and got an expert to appraise the stamps. None matched the Gronchi Rosa in value, but all together the stamps had been assessed at about forty-six thousand dollars. The sale had proceeded without a glitch.

Norman looked out the window and tried to conceal his laughter. He had not laughed since that fatal day when he had dropped the precious stamp into Theresa's pocket.

So that sweet, innocent-looking woman was a crook, and a clever one. Her plan had worked out perfectly. Kurt Todd could torture her and kill her, but he had no chance of recovering the stamp nor the money, since she had spent all of it. Besides, Theresa would have the law on her side. Everything she had done appeared to be legal. That was the best part of the entire rip-off. Norman laughed aloud, this time.

"What's the joke?" asked the passenger seated beside him.

"Joke? Oh...." He'd better get hold of himself. "Something funny that happened to me. Personal, though."

He unfolded the table in preparation for the meal. Time to enjoy the flight.

22

Vienna, December 2000

Exasperated Norman Arbib threw the little Collins English-German dictionary onto the hotel bed. He had not collected one single fact that added to what he already knew about the Gronchi Rosa sold in Austria. Theresa's lawyer in Krems, invoking client's privilege, had flatly refused to supply any information; the auctioneer in Vienna had only given him a cold look and a thick pamphlet. The pamphlet contained the long list of Theresa's stamps, which, of course, included the Gronchi Rosa. Neither man concealed annoyance with Norman's many questions. There was nothing they had to say and there was nothing they would say.

After three days Norman had changed strategy, and tried to get information on Theresa's late aunt. He had gone to the cemeteries in Krems; with a congruous donation for tombs without sponsors he had managed to look at the registry of the deceased. When he finally found a Theresia Albrecht, her death was dated two centures before.

Everything he did required an extraordinary amount of time and energy—posing a question took at least three tries, in which he mixed three words of German with ten of English since outside Vienna very few people spoke his language. *You can't play detective in a country without knowing the language,* Norman mused. *If I could find Theresa and follow her without being noticed—that would be a breakthrough, since she may lead me to a trail of useful connections.* But, if Theresa had been in Krems, nobody had seen her. In the present circumstance he wouldn't learn anything new about Theresa's role in the sale of the Gronchi Rosa. He had to decide what to do upon his return to Canada—give up Theresa and get Kurt Todd off his back or say that the sale had been done on behalf of an Austrian client in a perfectly legal manner. In fact, if it had not been for the confidential information he had extracted from Theresa, the transaction would appear to be an internal affair carried out within Austrian territory. There was a chance Todd would find out, though. The man was sharp as a whip and deadly as a mamba. Was Theresa worth the risk?

He'd make this decision later. Now it was time to enjoy his last two days in Vienna. He took a shower and dressed with an impeccable dark blue suit he had rented before leaving.

Time to see Vienna by night.

In the *Roter Salon* of the Altstadt Vienna Hotel, a pianist played one Viennese waltz after another. Sitting in front of a slice of a *Topfentorte* and a glass of *Traminer Spätweinlese*, Norman sipped with pleasure on his sweet wine.

It was then that he saw her.

Dressed in a green suit with black lapels, Theresa made a magnificent entrance, her red hair swaying with each step.

A waiter glided to welcome her and showed her to a table only a few feet from Norman.

He wanted to disappear, but it was too late. Theresa had seen him, and she was staring at him. He needed to improvise.

Norman rose slowly, neared Theresa's table, and bowed slightly. "The hotel manager was right," he said. "Sooner or later, every tourist ends up in this café. At least once." He gave her one of his award-winning smiles. "May I sit?" he asked.

Theresa nodded. "How come you're here?" she asked with a weak voice.

"I've been coming here at least once every day since last Sunday, hoping to see you." Theresa's pallor matched the white of the tablecloth. "I was laid off for a month. So I decided to follow a beautiful woman on her mysterious trip," he said.

"You mean you've come here *for me*?"

Acting with nonchalance was Norman's second nature. "What's strange about that? You left a message on my machine saying that you were taking a trip to Vienna. Isn't this place Vienna?" The color of her face had not changed. Clearly, Theresa did not believe a word he had said. He turned toward the waiter who had been standing by the table more than a few minutes, enthralled by the sight of Theresa. "Bring a slice of the cake you gave me, and some of that special wine. I'd like my friend to taste them both." He turned toward Theresa. "Maybe they will put you in the mood to waltz with me all night."

Theresa finished her cake very slowly and hardly touched her wine. "Dancing, you said? Maybe I should go change, put on a nice dress."

"Not for me," Norman replied. "Your suit is very becoming." Was she trying to get away? "We can go to a theatre, if you prefer."

"No, I love dancing…."

"Let's go, then." Resolutely Norman took the bill and paid.

At the dance hall Theresa spoke little, except to compliment the music or a tasty snack. Norman watched her carefully, still undecided. *No confrontation while in Austria*, he concluded. For any action, he needed Theresa to return home. So it was best to avoid making her more suspicious. Better play the man foolishly in love. "You didn't seem too pleased to see me here," he said. "I hope you don't think I was too forward." He paused. "I'd like you to know that I wouldn't have approached you, had I seen you in the company of a man."

Theresa shook her head. "I was just *very* surprised."

She never had much attention from men, Norman thought. Let's see if I can make her believe that she is so attractive that men would chase her across an ocean. He invited her to dance. "You must be accustomed to men following you," he said winking an eye.

"Well…not really."

"I'm prepared for tough competition, Theresa. I imagine you can have any man you want. I'm ready to fight to have a chance to be with you." An English waltz started and Theresa leaned against him. The girl was starved for affection and attention. It was going to be an easy game to make her believe that he had the hots for her. "I was surprised to find you here alone. Surprised, but pleased." He lifted her hair and kissed her neck. "You still didn't tell me why you came to Austria," he said. A bit of curiosity was the most natural feeling to display.

"Garments for Pleasure asked me to take my vacation time with little notice. For a while I had it in mind to come and see where my late aunt lived." As the band took a break, Norman and Theresa went back to their table. "I told you I had an aunt in Austria, haven't I?"

"Well, you mentioned something in your phone message, but I'd like to hear more about her." A measured interest was the proper reaction to her question.

"She was a very sweet old lady. She had no kids, and no other relatives but me. She left me all she had. It may not seem much to most people, but for me it was a fortune." She paused and sipped her peach snap. "I wanted to see where she lived. I went to a village near Krems, and gone by her house. I just wanted to have the feeling for the place. That was the main reason for my trip."

Norman anxiously waited for more, but Theresa quietly finished her drink.

"How long have you been in Vienna?"

"Only one day."

"That's why I didn't spot you before."

"I've been sick for three days. Because of change in food, I believe. But I'll come back. It's a wonderful city, and so much to see!"

"When do you leave?"

"Tomorrow morning."

"Oh, but that's too bad. I came here for you! I hoped we could spend some time together!"

"Well, my visit was a must-do visit. Maybe next time it will be pleasure only." She winked at him.

"Excellent idea."

"Well, time to hit the sack," she said looking at her watch. "I'm leaving early. When do you leave?"

"In two days. Unfortunately I can't change the return date without penalty, otherwise I'd love to fly back with you." He tried to guess her mood. The Theresa he had met in Toronto was different from the Theresa he was talking to. "I'll be back in time for our next cross-country appointment. Is it on, eh?"

"Of course. I wouldn't miss it for anything in the world." She rose. "Thank you for the wonderful evening. I really have to go. I'm very tired, and I still have to pack."

"Can I accompany you?"

Theresa nodded. "I'm staying at the Altstadt Vienna, the hotel where you found me."

Back in his room, Norman couldn't stop thinking of Theresa and her behavior. She was a real natural. She kept her cool, kind but distant. She was an experienced con artist. He jumped onto the bed and laughed inwardly: together, they were two of a kind!

23

From the large window of his office Chief Detective Conrad Miguel Tormez watched the glazers leaving the premises. The addition to the police station, designated to house a forensic lab, was finally completed. The new equipment had already arrived and would be installed soon. This expansion was important, since it would avoid shuffling samples to be tested back and forth the station. The computer group had moved into the new wing a week ago.

Unfortunately the presence of modern investigative means was the only positive thing Conrad could think about. His boss was getting nervous, and he was not the calmest person in the world to start with. For the last week he had hammered him with questions about Operation Woman in Black. Conrad had managed to keep him at bay, since the expenses incurred by Savina in the Virgin Islands were paid by Denis Taillard. But he worried, too. He had not planned a rushed operation, since it wouldn't look real, but he did not want things to be dragged on either. The longer Savina was involved in the operation, the higher was the risk that the operation blew apart.

And there was another worry. Every time he called Savina, Denis came on the phone, and all Denis had to say was that everything was progressing well. Progressing! Nothing was moving, that was the truth! All Savina had to do was to dive into bed and make that famous tape. That shouldn't have taken long.

He tried to figure out what had happened. With good intentions, maybe Denis had displayed a great deal of charm trying to make Savina happy in an attempt to compensate her for the risks she was taking. Perhaps Savina, in spite of his instructions and advice, had been drawn to all the glitter money can buy: the luxury accommodations, the tropical enchantment, the exotic food, the leisure time at the beach…and a man eager to please her.

111

Conrad was ready to place another call to Denis, when Rudy came up the stairs. He gave him a thick envelope. "Mr. Taillard's chauffeur delivered this for you, Sir. He said I had to give it to you in person."

Eagerly Conrad fingered the envelope: it contained a tape! Without saying a word he went to the projection room.

He played the VHS tape. For the next twenty minutes Conrad watched it carefully. It looked good. But he had to be sure. He rewound it and went to grab a coffee. He sat in a chair, and watched the tape again. Only Denis' voice was distinguishable, all other noises were little gasps or strong moans. *Good*, he thought. Then he studied Savina's positions. Her face was always hidden; the hand with Clara's ring clasped Denis' shoulder or caressed his arm. *Great*. He rewound it and played it again, to be sure that Clara's old tapes had not been left lying around. There weren't any. The actors had worked carefully. He rewound the tape and played it for the fourth time to judge the level of sexual involvement. It was convincing, he decided. All he had to do was to sanitize it of fingerprints and ship it to the post box address left on Clara's recording machine.

He rubbed his hands together. At last the trap was set. Whoever picked up the tape should lead him to the mastermind of the criminal ring.

No doubt his boss would be very pleased.

At mid afternoon he placed a call to Bernice.

"A candlelight dinner?" Bernice asked. "What's the occasion?"

Conrad jiggled the phone from one hand to the other. "Won't tell you. It's a surprise. Do I get a yes?" Conrad knew the answer already. Bernice had been a discreet, caring friend. A widow of a man with a bad temper, Bernice had found herself alone in raising a teenager who had inherited some of his father's bad traits. As soon as she had moved next door, Bernice had taken a liking to Isabel, teaching her knitting and basket-weaving. Early in the morning the three of them—Conrad, Isabel and Bernice—often went jogging. Isabel, tall for her age and fast like a deer, would run ahead then back to join them.

"Six o'clock. I booked at the Budapest Inn," Conrad said.

Bernice laughed. "I'll be ready."

Conrad and Bernice arrived early and for a while they were the only patrons. Their table, set in a corner of the restaurant, glowed with candlelight and music played in the background. They glanced at the menu and exchanged opinion on a variety of dishes, as they indulged in their second martini. Then Bernice leaned toward Conrad and asked him, "So what's the occasion?" Her short silver hair framed her perfect oval face, and a soft pink blouse flattered her creamy complexion.

"The occasion? Ah, yes…would you like to marry me? I'd planned to ask you a long time ago. I was just waiting to have some time off. But now…."

"Yes, yes, yes!" Bernice cut in. She winked at him. "I wanted to have a chance to answer!"

Conrad laughed. "Wait! There's a string attached to the proposal. I'd like to become the guardian of Isabel's child." He tried to read her mind. "How do you feel about it?"

"You know I like children. I enjoyed my Jerome a lot. I do even now that he's giving me problems." She lifted her brown eyes to look at Conrad. "I'd be happy to help you out with Isabel and Junior."

Conrad stretched forward to kiss her on the lips; he then raised his glass. "To our life together. I always have a great time with you, Bernice. You like to stay home, and I love to have somebody waiting for me at night." He paused. "I already talked to my lawyer about getting custody of Junior. He doesn't foresee any problem. However, he said, things would move faster if I was married."

The waiter came to take their orders. "Grilled chicken with steamed vegetables," Bernice said.

"Make it two," Conrad said.

"How come you passed on the steak tartare?"

Conrad sighed. "I need to lose weight. As you have probably noticed, now Isabel makes almost three rounds when we go jog. She makes me feel much older than my fifty years."

A week later Conrad and Bernice were ready to pronounce their vows. Morning rays seeped into the chapel as Conrad and Bernice, hand in hand, walked through the center aisle. Two tripods loaded with cascades of white gladiolas and carnations flanked the small altar, one on each side. The minister of the United Church, holding a missal in his hands, welcomed them with a warm smile.

Isabel, with Junior in her arms, took a seat on the left; Jerome sat on the right-hand side; Rudy Ashwald, the witness, stood behind the bride and groom.

Bernice adjusted the belt of her pale-blue dress and shifted the bouquet of white roses from one hand to the other. She was impatient for the ceremony to start. For a long time she had waited and hoped for this important moment. In Conrad she had found all the support a person could get from another human being, and the hours spent with him had been the most serene of her life.

The minister's words slithered over her like pleasant, soft music. She wanted to keep her cool during the entire ceremony. She tried to concentrate on the stained glass windows behind the altar, representing Christ's passion. But when she heard the minister say, "And now I pronounce you man and wife," she erupted into tears.

Conrad cupped her waist with his arm and pulled her close. He whispered in her ear, "You never told me it would be such a painful thing getting married to me!" He looked down on her with love.

Bernice quickly dried her eyes and leaned against him. "Just happy, that's all."

* * *

His feet, totally immersed in the deep snow, were freezing, but Al Garnett wanted to see what was going on. Standing on his tiptoes he flattened his cheek against one of the chapel's lateral windows. Peeking between two colored figures in the stained glass, he managed to get a view of the interior.

So Conrad Tormez was getting married to the woman who refused to let him in the house...now, now, things were getting serious. That woman would be on guard all the time. His chances of paying a visit to Isabel would be slimmer than before. He had to think of something else to reach his girl.

But now it was time to go back to Kurt Todd's house in the hills. His boss had probably checked on him more than once.

* * *

Alone in his refuge on Lake Erie, Kurt Todd kept shifting in his chair. No way to deny it, he was nervous. He had tried to forget about the two operations that had failed, and forced himself to concentrate on the ones on the go. He wondered now...did those two old operations interfere with the new ones? Did they provide the police with critical information about his organization? In the back of his mind he felt that there was something subtle but dangerous that was ready to explode. *A premonition, maybe?* Things were not going as smoothly as in the past. Experience had taught him that a successful operation had to be swift, and must follow a precise, rigorous script. Clara Moffatt had moved her vacation from Jamaica to the Virgin Islands without a convincing explanation, and she was supposed to have made the compromising tape involving Denis Taillard days ago; instead she was not back yet. Norman Arbib had stayed in Austria longer than agreed upon and he had not come to see him, rattling off one excuse after another. To make things worse, Al Garnett was not answering the phone. He only hoped that Garnett was not wandering in town, risking recognition by the police.

For the first time since he had built his rocky refuge, Todd felt confined in the small area clogged with all sorts of equipment. He wished he could leave and take some time off.

To calm himself he went on the Internet and logged into the chat room of the group known as *Disguises at Work*. The annual fee for that club was astronomical, but it was the best online resource describing the latest findings on how to portray another person, together with their rate of success.

He was familiar with all the items listed, except one. He clicked on that hot link, and found himself looking at one of the Web pages of McGill University.

24

The past week had been filled with action and emotional stress, but now it was time to relax. Conrad got a Labatt Blue from the fridge and tuned into the Sports Channel. There was no better way to spend a Saturday afternoon than watching a football game. He had just adjusted his recliner when the phone rang. It was his cellular, so he knew the call was from the station. He set the remote on mute and turned on his cellular. "Yes," he said at length.

"It's Rudy, Sir."

Normally Rudy would begin by apologizing for something for which he was not responsible or by expressing regrets to have called him at home. But he did not. *Bad news*, Conrad mused instantly.

"An urgent message from the lab, Sir. It's about Pappa-pappa."

"Yes?" Rudy did not utter a word. "Yes! What about it?" Since the tape had been delivered, Conrad had not been concerned about the speech transposer or Savina. He was just waiting for the tape to be picked up.

"Pappa-pappa isn't the only system that can emulate other people's speech. There is a similar program on the Internet that can be downloaded free." Rudy paused as if afraid to continue. "The lab is testing it." He paused again. "They told me to inform you immediately."

He had expected problems with the use of the speech transposer, but surely not a duplication of it, available to everybody! And this just after he had sent the tape off.

"Mr. Tormez?" Rudy asked. "Are you still there? Are you okay?"

"Yes. Just shocked. I didn't expect anything of this sort." If anybody else had been on the phone, he would not hesitate to swear. But Rudy was a gentleman in police clothes: he couldn't do that to him. "Be right there," he said curtly.

Savina's life could be in danger.

"Cookies?" Conrad asked. He let himself land in one of the chairs available. There was more to learn, and all that computer stuff did not interest him in the least.

The computer analyst, Jeff Williams, nodded and started one of his monologues. Jeff weighed at least three hundred pounds, he had bushy hair, and his eyeglasses miraculously stood on the tip of his nose. The chair he was sitting in totally disappeared behind his body. Jeff was a nice fellow, competent, and eager to help. But explaining things was not his cup of tea. Conrad waited patiently. His only defense was to ask questions, and force Jeff to give him a specific answer. When Jeff stopped talking for a second, Conrad interjected, "So you contacted the author of this new package and found she's monitoring the number of people accessing her Web page, is this correct?"

"Yes. She wants to keep count of how many people download her software. But that isn't all." He paused. "She has built an interactive utility...." He didn't finish since Conrad put up a hand. "Sorry, Conrad. I'll rephrase. Every time somebody clicks on her Web page, her computer grabs the Internet identity of the user and stores it in a file."

"Oh, smart!"

Jeff smiled. "In this way she has a record of the interaction between her PC and the computer that accesses her Web page. She also asks for the user's screen name. But that is not a condition for downloading her software."

"I see. Did you tell her we're testing her work?"

Jeff smiled again. "She knew we were the first to download her package." He paused, uncertain. "I knew the situation was critical for your operation. I took the liberty of asking her to forward us a daily update of her records. I hope you don't mind my initiative."

Conrad finally relaxed against the chair. "Mind, you said? Damned grateful! At least we can keep an eye on the people interested in speech transposing."

Conrad spent the entire evening pondering the consequences of the availability of the new speech emulator. He had to talk to Savina and explain to her the danger the new software package posed. If only

117

she and Denis had not spent all that extra time in the Virgin Islands! He waited until morning then called Denis' house. He asked for Savina, but he couldn't shake Denis off the phone.

"What's this urgency all about? What's the problem?" Denis asked.

"You!" Conrad couldn't control his anger. It was worse than that, *he did not want to control it.* "You should have known better than to stay away two and half weeks!" he shouted into the phone. "What have you two been doing? You were part of a police operation. You weren't supposed to be honeymooning!"

Denis calmly accepted his friend's explosion. "Conrad, try to understand. It wasn't easy to make the tape to start with. There was no director or photographer to advise us. We only had a sheet with your instructions."

"So—" Conrad barked into the phone. "You only had to follow them! One week should have been plenty!" Clearly, the two had spent their time fucking each other. After all the recommendations he had made to Savina! "Let me talk to Savina."

"She's in the shower. Conrad, the tape should be in your hands by now. There's nothing to be upset about." He paused. "Look at it, it's almost as good as the two Clara made."

Conrad had watched it four times. It was good, all right. Pressed to conclude the operation, he had rushed the tape to its destination, which was the address left on Clara's recording machine. Now that he knew about the new speech transposer, he regretted having acted so fast. "The tape is okay." Of course it was okay, the two actors had probably practiced the scene dozens of times! He tried to keep his voice even. "But we have another problem. A big one." He paused for effect. "I need to talk to Savina. It's urgent. Get her out of the shower."

"You can tell me what you want to tell Savina," Denis said calmly.

Great. The two were an item, now. This was going to be another complication and only God knew in how much hot water he already was. "Okay, okay. Come over here then, the two of you. As soon as possible. But tell Savina that what I feared it might happen has indeed occurred. She should get ready for it." He rang off.

* * *

118

When Savina came out of the shower, Denis patted the bed. "Come to sit by me, Savina."

Her body folded in a huge terrycloth housecoat, Savina looked like a teenager who badly needed protection. He had trusted the danger was over. But then what was Conrad blathering about? "What did Conrad tell you that he didn't tell me? He mentioned something that he feared could happen." Savina lowered your eyes. "I thought everything was going to be back to normal the moment the tape was delivered. The delivery of the tape was supposed to provide Conrad with the lead he desperately needed." As Savina did not meet his eyes, Denis lifted her chin. "I want to know."

Savina sighed. "It's better if you don't," she muttered.

"We're in this together." He kissed her on the tip of her button nose. "I want to know everything that involves you or me."

"Conrad told me that if anybody got wind of the existence of the speech emulator, I'd have to go into hiding."

"Conrad never mentioned any of this to me!"

"He was afraid you wouldn't agree. But he assured me the odds were low."

Denis rose and paced the bedroom for a while. He stopped in front of Savina. "Conrad is going to hear from me! That's for sure. Let's get dressed and go see him at the station."

25

Conrad was haunted by his find: the voice-disguising system used by Savina was not a secret invention to be used and tested by the police, but knowledge available to millions of people. Information on the new system could appear on any computer monitor in the world at the click of a mouse.

The experts at the police lab had evaluated the efficiency of the new system and tried to measure the danger it posed to Savina's cover. Savina.... What he, Conrad, had mentioned to her as a remote possibility was now an impelling necessity. She would have to live in seclusion for some time, until the net closed on the criminal ring.

He actually had no power to impose any action on Savina or Denis because they were citizens cooperating with police. His boss may have been right after all, when he almost refused to approve Operation Woman in Black. His boss...he would have to face him to ask for additional funds to finance Savina's new identity and temporary hiding.

And that after he had blown his top over the bill for Savina's new wardrobe.

A man's and a woman's footsteps resounded distinctly on the congoleum floor: Savina and Denis had arrived. They soberly greeted Conrad and took seats, holding hands across the chairs' armrests. Savina looked withdrawn, in contrast with Denis' aggressive appearance.

"Explain this story about Savina having to go in hiding," Denis brusquely said. "She knew of it before the operation started, but you never told me a word about it."

It was true. He had advised Savina but not Denis, thinking that the problem would not matter to him. He never suspected Denis would fall in love with a woman of low social status. Everybody knew Denis was a good soul but the snob of the snobs.

Conrad pondered his answer. "At that time," he said slowly, "that remote possibility concerned only Savina." He looked at Denis, almost imploringly. "Bear with me, Denis. I try to foresee things when dealing with an operation as complex as Woman in Black. I didn't even imagine you falling for Savina so…so deeply. I suspected she could fall for you, so I preached to her not to get emotionally involved." He looked at Savina, who held Denis' hand tight, then at Denis. He had never seen two human beings so close to each other. He surely did not need that extra complication. He resumed talking, "I took all precautions to protect Savina and make the operation a success."

Conrad suspended his explanation, watching its effect on Denis. He seemed appeased a bit, but only a bit. Using the most dramatic tone he could muster, he said, "Savina is in deep danger."

"Meaning what?" Denis asked.

Conrad cleared his throat. "Let me back up a little. The speech transposer we used was a new discovery in the process of being patented. We got this prototype from the inventor himself. Pappa-pappa was implemented entirely in hardware with DPS. These are fast chips: each instruction is executed in a few nanoseconds. A nanosecond is a billionth of a second—this resulted in an incredibly fast processing of the input voice, which is the voice of the person one wants to disguise." Conrad paused. "Now," he said exhaling deeply, "somebody has come up with a similar system, implemented in software. You'd think it's much slower, but it isn't so. It's slightly slower, true, but much richer in vocabulary. Groups of words commonly used are stored in memory; these groups can be accessed extremely fast using look-up tables."

"How is it possible?" Denis asked.

"This new system makes use of high-speed static RAM. Just recently, this kind of memory became affordable." Conrad paused again. "The package is available on the Internet. It's public domain."

"When did it appear?"

"Only five days ago. Its author is a student at McGill University. She designed it, implemented it, and published the results as part of

121

her degree. She won a prize for that. Last week. It's all on the home page of Jeanne Michelle Leaumont."

For a moment nobody spoke, then Denis broke the ice. "Do you really believe that they, the bad guys I mean, would spend their time looking for these kinds of inventions?"

"Yes. I believe they would. They are always interested in impersonating somebody else. I'm sure that sooner or later they will discover this new system and run a few tests on it. There are plenty of groups collecting information on disguises; they make them available to their members—for a fee, of course."

"If they don't know of the existence of a hardware companion, Savina is safe." Denis commented.

"Things aren't that simple. There's more. More complications, I mean."

"Which are?" asked Denis.

"The student took a further step. She tested her software extensively. She examined the frequency spectrum resulting from the words spoken by the speech transposer and compared it with that of real people. About three hundred cases. The two spectra are similar, of course, but the artificial one, obtained through the speech device, is smoother and more uniform than the real one." Conrad stopped, exhausted. It took him five hours to understand how this new system worked, and he wasn't sure he could explain it to others. "Do you get the idea?" he asked.

"Vaguely," replied Denis.

"We can go to the lab and see the system in operation," suggested Conrad.

"Later, maybe," Denis said dryly.

"There is more...." said Conrad. "Leaumont has defined a measure to compare these two mysterious spectra. Accurately."

"Meaning—" said Denis.

"As soon as we got hold of the new system, we used Leaumont's measure to test our data. The fake words spoken by our Woman in Black generate a pattern much flatter than the words spoken by Clara Moffatt."

"That's still a long way to find my girl."

"Not really. Savina has left plenty of messages on her machine. That was their order; the order that sparked the idea of replacing

Clara with Savina since Savina wouldn't have to answer on the spot. We know that those messages were taped by the listener." Conrad sighed. "Unfortunately they have several messages they can use to run a comparison. And if they do, they will know they've been entrapped, that the recent Woman in Black was an impostor."

Nobody spoke for a while. Then Denis and Savina whispered to each other.

"We don't believe in this great impending danger," Denis said gravely. "Savina and I will go to my mother's place and stay there."

"Denis—" started Conrad.

"I listened to you once. I accepted involvement in a project that was foolish. Insane. Absurd. You assured me there were no loose ends." Denis looked at Conrad defiantly. "I really don't feel like trusting you again."

"Denis," said Conrad, and then, "Savina," he said almost begging, "please listen to me. If they find out the truth, they only have to take a look at you to know who impersonated Clara Moffatt, even if you reassume your own appearance."

Denis did not leave any time for Savina to reply. "Don't try to convince Savina of your new project. The seclusion bit. Savina stays with me. If she goes into hiding, you may convince her once more to help you out to catch the mastermind of the operation. I'm starting to figure out how ruthless you really are."

Denis' remark hurt him so much that Conrad remained speechless.

"You justify everything with the excuse of doing your job," continued Denis. "You don't hesitate to risk people's lives to reach your goal." Turning to Savina he said, "We've listened to enough nonsense for one day. Let's go."

26

Conrad got a glass of water and sipped on it slowly, trying to wash away the taste of bitterness.

It was then that Rudy Ashwald rushed into his office, his cheeks red, a big smile on his face. "Fred Kusteroff has picked up the envelope with the tape. He seems to be heading home. An unmarked car is following him."

Conrad sprang to his feet. That was the break he needed. He began shouting orders, dispatching two teams to Kusteroff's house. "Get a chopper too," he commanded. "That place is near the lake. I want to cover the possibility of a boat ready to take off." He went to brief his boss, then grabbed his coat and left.

"Mr. Tormez," said a feminine voice behind him, "Is it true that you've cracked the case of the sex blackmailers?"

Conrad shot her a penetrating look. Who in the world had leaked that information? He did not need a reporter to broadcast that a police raid was in progress. It would endanger the success of the operation altogether. He forced a smile. "Not really. But we're working on the case."

"Where are you heading?" the same voice asked. The woman followed him. Clearly she had not seen his men taking off at record speed; otherwise she would be already on their tails. Maybe he could try a diversion. The woman was quite young. With a flirty gesture he straightened his tie knot and gave her a smile of complicity. "I'm going to a cottage on the lake," he said. "Care to join me for a weekend of pleasure?"

The reporter blushed and shook her head.

Thank God for shy women, Conrad thought as he swiftly walked to his car.

Conrad parked his vehicle close to the others and reached the clearing on foot. His men were already in tactical position, two on top of the near rock overlooking the lake, the other six forming a semicircle around Kusteroff's cottage, well sheltered by trees and evergreens.

Conrad kept the radio in his hand, ready to give orders. They could burst into Kusteroff's house and arrest him. But the cottage location made him suspicious. There could be more than one player. He waited and made his men wait for about an hour.

It was dusk when Kusteroff came out of the house and stood in front of the northern side of a rock. "Close in," Conrad ordered to the six men positioned around the area. "Don't make any noise. Somebody is bound to show up. Shoot only if necessary."

Slowly an opening appeared in the rocky wall. As Kusteroff entered it, two of Conrad's men pushed their way in while another two forced the door to remain open.

Conrad rushed inside.

The silhouette of a tall man appeared in the background. Two policemen handcuffed Kusteroff and took the envelope containing the tape out of his hands.

With a somersault the tall man tumbled out of the room. A door in the back wall of the corridor swung open and reclosed behind him.

"We need a lock-pick gun," said one of the policemen as soon as he realized that the door was locked. "I'll go get it. I have it in the trunk of my car."

Conrad walked out and ordered the two men still outside to head for the lakeshore. Their target was clearly heading that way. He then joined his men inside, and waited for the door to be opened. When finally that happened, they stood in front of an elevator carved in the mossy rock.

"We won't be able to use it," Conrad shouted. "Our man has probably disabled the command." He contacted the chopper. "Stay on guard. At least one man is heading for shore. He may try to take off, if our crew doesn't stop him before." To the officers around him, he said, "Let's go outside and reach the lakeshore on foot."

Conrad worried. *Do I he have enough manpower?* When they had surrounded Fred Kusteroff's house he thought somebody would wait until dark to come get the tape. He never suspected that there could be an operative center totally carved in a rock, only fifty feet from Kusteroff's house!

There could not be a better place to run a clandestine operation. A no-exit gravel road leading to the center guaranteed lack of traffic and a waterway fifty feet down the cliff offered an easy exit by boat. Around that cliff there was one bay after another, some not easy to spot either from shore or from the lake. *The place had been well chosen*, Conrad mused. To make the situation worse the shores, continually eroded by the waves, had become little strips of sand, flanked, on the northern side, by small hills reachable only by small, steep trails. All these features created an ideal condition for a criminal to escape. And now it was dusk—an unwanted aggravation, since nobody had thought of getting the goggles for night vision.

Conrad quickened his steps and finally reached the little bay at the foot of the rock. The tall man was still at large; the helicopter was circling over the area. "What happened?" he asked the two officers who had preceded him on shore.

"We heard the clatter of elevator doors. When we went near it, we couldn't see anybody. From the chopper circling above we know nobody moved out of the bay or climbed the rock. We're still searching. But it's getting dark."

Conrad's keen eyes surveyed the surface of the surrounding rocks. Nothing moved. He turned and scrutinized the bay. In spite of the advanced season a boat was still in the waters. At first glance the boat seemed securely moored to the dock, but when he focused his eyes on it, Conrad realized that the boat swayed, gliding on the water and smoothly clearing its way among the few ice slabs. "The boat!" he shouted. "The man is under water, trying to guide the boat away from here. Get him! Quick!"

Two officers dove close to the boat; one emerged with a long rope, the other surfaced here and there, struggling with the man. Conrad did not have to issue any order—two more officers joined the fight.

A few minutes later the man, dripping water from head to toe, was handcuffed.

In the darkness of night, the tall man repeated: "My name is Kurt Todd, and my address is 26 Nunavut Avenue, Toronto." His voice sounded familiar, Conrad thought. "According to the Charter of Rights that's all I have to say."

Just what society needs. Educated criminals, Conrad thought in a flash. "That's right, Mr. Todd," he said aloud, then paused. "But you'll find it more convenient to talk to save your skin, that is if you aren't the mastermind of the sex scandals." He would have given him his intimidating cross-eyed look except it was too dark for the man to see it.

He turned away from Todd. "Bring him in," Conrad said to Chris Vannini, the young officer closest to him. "Two of you come with me. We need to go through all the material Todd has been keeping in his hideout. The others can go home."

It took Conrad only an hour to realize that they had hit the core of the criminal organization. He tracked down names and addresses of Todd's men. He immediately dispatched new teams to their residences. An invisible net was going to be cast on them at the same time, in the middle of the night, making escape impossible.

Exhilaration was getting hold of him. After months of delays, setbacks, and frustrations, all of them would fall into the hands of the law. He closed his eyes. Everything had gone so well he couldn't believe it.

The event called for celebration. He phoned home and asked his family to join him for a late supper at the Amalfi restaurant. He had gone without food for more than sixteen hours.

But before putting his car in gear, he should give the good news to Savina. He dialed the Taillard's number and left a message for her: Operation Woman in Black had succeeded. Savina was finally free; she would have nothing more to fear.

27

On the shore of Lake Erie

Ron Donavan did not like what Todd had ordered him to do. For years he had complied with everything Todd had wanted, but now...the request to dress up a belt with plastic worried him tremendously. Imported explosive material, Todd had specified. Stunned and mumbling, Ron had asked what that item would be used for, since he wanted to know what was on Todd's mind. As far as he knew, Todd had kept himself clear of murder.

Todd had thrown back his head and laughed—that mean laughter he had developed in the last few months. "Protection, my dear man, simple and pure protection. At times I need to scare some people to death," Todd had replied.

Hesitantly yet afraid of being Todd's first victim, Donavan had complied. His boss brooked neither disobedience nor defection.

It had taken more than a month to find explosive that couldn't be traced, but today he had received from Northern Ireland a small quantity of PETN. It was all he needed. Alone in his shack he slipped on a pair of surgical gloves. He grabbed the belt Todd had given him and turned it upside down a couple of times. It had an interior like a money belt; it was wide and made of strong but soft leather. The top of the buckle opened to reveal a small box. Ron looked at Todd's specifications. Simple in theory, they were difficult to implement. As usual, Todd didn't show any understanding of how complicated it was to build a bomb that could fit in a small space; and Todd never grasped the concept that no part of a bomb could be easily tested— surely no part of this one. Ron got hold of a microchip, some hair-thin

128

wire, and a cellular phone from which he had extracted the mouthpiece. He began to work.

When he was finished the belt contained the phone. One single ring would trigger the detonator and bring swift death to its wearer.

Ron Donavan drove to Todd's new house. As he arrived, he exchanged a few words with Al Garnett. He then deposited the belt in the basement with a big sign *cellular* on top of it, as he had been instructed. He was in a rush to leave, to avoid having Garnett ask him for a ride to Varlee. On his way home he stopped in downtown Toronto to catch a late show at Silver City. Waiting for the show to commence, he stood in front of a TV set, a Guinness beer in one hand and a bag of popcorn in the other. It was at that precise moment that the news of the police raid on Todd's rocky hideout began to unfold.

Donavan did not wait for the program to finish. He quickly deposited his beer on the counter and strode out. He was tempted to retrace his steps and retrieve the item he had just delivered. He was the only member of Todd's gang capable of combining explosives with electronics to create small but effective bombs. As he entered his car, however, the idea of distancing himself from anything that could link him to Kurt Todd prevailed.

He would drive west and reach the Rockies. He knew of a mountain cabin that would provide him with a safe shelter—at least for a few weeks.

28

The royal palace and the art gallery Norman Arbib had visited in Vienna held no name in his memory, but they had left him with a sense of grandiosity and harmony. He had never seen anything of that kind. He stayed in Vienna until running out of money, since he was not eager to return home and face Kurt Todd. He couldn't come to a decision about the information he had collected on Theresa.

Norman opened the door of his apartment and slid his duffle bag onto the floor. A smell of old rugs hit his nostrils. What a terrible dump his home was!

He grabbed a cold beer from the fridge and sipped it as he walked into the small living room. He lifted a cushion from the sofa. Springs had pierced the underlying fabric and the stuffing had burst at the cushion seams. He shoved the stuffing in and put the cushion back in place. He should take action; make a radical change in his life. Crime had not been profitable for him. He stretched out on the sofa and turned on the TV. Time to catch up with the latest news.

Kurt Todd's arrest took a great portion of the news. Todd's life unrolled before Norman's eyes: Todd, the alleged mastermind of the sex blackmails; Todd, the expert forger of official documents; Todd, suspected of having stolen valuable stamps from rich collectors.

The anchorman went on and on, saying that Todd's top men had been arrested, too, but he did not give any names. The police operation, which had taken months of preparation and the use of sophisticated technology, had succeeded completely and should be considered closed.

When he heard the last sentence Norman felt enormous relief. Perhaps it was his golden opportunity to pull out of a business he had come to hate. But his relief was short lived. He knew enough about police matters to realize that the authorities would never stop looking for possible criminal connections. He should still watch over his shoulder.

But at least Kurt Todd was off his back.

The following morning he called Theresa. She sounded cold, distant. Given the circumstances, he understood her reticence. But things had taken a different turn, now. With Todd out of circulation, he could court her for what she was: an attractive woman whose company he earnestly enjoyed. He would never find another Theresa.

He invited her for a run on the cross-country trails.

"Well...I heard there isn't much snow left. And I feel quite tired. A bug of some sort."

"What about a nice lunch at The Hermitage, then, tomorrow? Quiet and relaxing. Tuesday is their slow day." Tuesday was Theresa's day off. As she did not reply, Norman continued, "Theresa, I really would like to see you, even if only for a short time. I can pick you up at eleven o'clock and take you back right after lunch. You'll have all afternoon to rest."

"Fine," she finally said.

The Christmas decorations looked almost out of season, so little snow was on the ground and so bright was the late morning sun. But The Hermitage had staged a superb show to draw its customers into the Christmas spirit.

Santa Claus's sled, pulled by six reindeer, circled the building, sliding over humps and gullies of artificial snow. With one hand Santa held the reins, with the other he waved at the crowd. Small snowmen in different costumes flanked both sides of the external stairway leading to the solarium.

Built like an ancient castle—three stories, stone walls, and pinnacles on each and every window of the top floor—The Hermitage was a massive yet elegant construction. A gym, a pool, a sauna, and a beauty parlor were part of the many facilities it offered to its exclusive clientele. The flat ceiling of the restaurant formed the support for the floor of the solarium, where tables and easy chairs were an invitation to relax.

In the middle of the solarium stood a gigantic pine tree sprinkled with white foam and loaded with garlands and tiny flickering candles.

Savina was admiring it, when Denis, standing behind her, asked, "Happy?" He hugged Savina, who turned to face him.

"Very. It was nice of you to take me to such an awesome place." She cupped his neck with her hands and planted a big kiss on his cheek.

"You're tickling my neck," Denis said. He took Savina's hands and pulled on her ruffled cuffs. "You should get rid of all these black clothes."

"First thing in the morning, I'll buy myself a new outfit. Bright blue. Too bad I can't go shopping at Garments for Pleasure. All employees get a 30% discount."

"I can ask Veronica to take you to one of her fancy shops."

"Great." Savina fingered her blond, straight hair. "After all, Conrad handled everything well."

"But he got my cooperation upon false premises," Denis said sharply. "I don't like people who tell me only half of the truth."

Savina shrugged. "Things worked out all right for me. I got a nice vacation and met a wonderful man."

"Nice to hear that, Savina." He took her hand. "Like to take a stroll on the beach?" A hundred feet away a pond shone under the sun, small chunks of ice floating on the water.

It was then that the sound of an ancient bell announced the opening of the restaurant. "Better not," Savina said. "We should get something to eat right away. My appointment with the hairstylist is for one o'clock sharp. Finally I'll be able to reassume my old appearance."

Theresa's brown leather coat was open, disclosing a green miniskirt and a great pair of legs. "Maybe we shouldn't walk on the beach," Norman said. "Your boots may get dirty."

"Oh no. Let's go. I'll dust off the sand later." Theresa linked her arm with Norman's and began walking on the shore. "I'd like to ask you a question, Norman, and you have to tell me the truth. What's your interest in me?"

Norman stopped cold. "You ask? Don't you know you're a very attractive woman?"

"Yes, but…I can't believe anybody would follow me to Austria, just to see me for a few hours!"

"Believe it, Theresa. I had hoped to spend a few days with you in Vienna. That didn't work out, unfortunately." He paused. "The truth is that I'm crazy about you! Just look at you, with that skirt and that tight top!"

Theresa laughed and shook her mass of red hair.

"I took my camera with me. So when you aren't around, I can still look at you." He gestured her to walk toward the pond. "Let me take a few pictures." He looked into the viewfinder and said, "Farther, Theresa, so I can get those seagulls sharing the water with the ice slabs. They make for an unusual backdrop." He clicked once then again. "Done. Tomorrow I'll know if my talent as a photographer has done justice to your beauty." He took her arm and led her toward the building.

Gingerly they entered the restaurant.

In front of them stood Savina and Denis, ready to be seated.

Theresa hesitated at first then went up to Savina. "I thought you were on a big trip!" She threw her arms around her and said to Norman, "This is the friend I told you so much about, Savina Thompson, the security guard at Garments for Pleasure." She turned toward Savina. "How come you're here, and what did you do to your beautiful hair?"

For a moment Savina froze. She never thought she could meet anybody who knew her at a fancy place like The Hermitage, least of all Theresa Albrecht, who was very careful about money. She should have known better than to show her face in public. "It's a long story," she finally mumbled. "I'll call you and tell you everything, Theresa. Soon." She took Denis' arm and pulled him close to her. She introduced him.

"Norman Arbib," Norman said in response, and stared at her.

Savina shot a big smile at Norman and winked at Theresa. "You'll have to excuse us. Right now Denis and I have some urgent matters to attend to."

Theresa hugged her again and told her, "Call me soon, Savina, or I'll die of curiosity."

In no time Denis and Savina were out of sight.

"That was weird," Theresa said. "She told everybody she was going on a big trip, and where do I find her? Only thirty miles from her apartment!"

"Weird," echoed Norman. "But let's think about us. The chef is a friend of mine. We're his guests. Order whatever you want and the fanciest drink you like." He smiled at Theresa. "I missed you. I hope we can spend time together."

PART 4

29

Jamaica, end of December 2000

Faithful to his policeman habits, Conrad surveyed his surroundings. On the left, the sandy shores stretched out of sight, on the right Isabel and Jerome were playing water volleyball under Bernice's attentive eyes. A huge umbrella made entirely of palm leaves sheltered Junior, who was taking a nap. A second, small, colorful umbrella was wide open on top of his buggy. His eyelashes, thickened by the sunscreen Bernice had spread all over his body, seemed stuck to his face. No chance that even the meanest sunray could harm him.

Bobo stopped licking his sore paws to emit a soft *arf*. Too late he had discovered that the sand was too hot for his delicate puppy's skin. Conrad scooped the dog into the crook of his arm and took him inside the cottage. With some effort he made him sit on the bathroom counter. He had just put ointment on one paw, when Bobo began licking it. After a few tries, Conrad decided it was a lost cause; maybe he would be able to medicate him when he fell asleep.

Carrying Bobo in one arm and a CD player in the other, Conrad returned to the beach and took a seat under the umbrella. Everything was in order. Time to relax and listen to some music since his stay would soon be over.

He had not expected his boss to be so prompt and generous. After he had received the news of Todd's capture, he had offered him a week's vacation that Conrad could take immediately. Combined with Christmas and the weekends, that resulted in a two-week holiday. He remembered how hard the word Christmas had hit him. The complex police Operation Woman in Black, Savina's precarious situation, his marriage to Bernice, and Isabel's problems had erased any notion of time and season from his mind. Without delay Bernice had come to his rescue. All of a sudden flyers advertising excursions, cruises, and holiday tours littered every corner of the house. Within a couple of hours a vacation spot was chosen, and a day later all suitcases were packed. The small cottage cost him a fortune but guaranteed his family plenty of privacy in spite of being located near the resort areas of Montego Bay.

Conrad pushed down on his chaise longue, took Bobo in his lap, and turned on the CD player. As the notes of *Spanish Eyes* began resounding, Conrad's mind plunged into the nebulous depths of his past.

He was only nineteen when he had danced to that beat one last time....

30

Silvaplana, California
Thirty-one years before

Driving an old Mustang, Dale Vernon and Conrad Tormez had gone to California to have a good time. Six-two and skinny with deep blue eyes and short spiky hair, Vernon exuded dynamism and efficiency. Tormez, heavyset and just over six feet tall, had a dark complexion with brown eyes and dark, thick hair. His measured gestures and his calm manners conveyed a feeling of strength. Dale, twenty-one, and Conrad, nineteen, had worked in construction for ten long weeks in order to afford a full month of fun and adventure. It was going to be their last holiday before entering the Police College in Aylmer. Ramon Gonzales, a constable with the Silvaplana police department and Tormez' uncle, had provided them with cheap accommodations at the Bluewater Motel right on the beach, where the action was.

The vacation was coming to an end. In a few days they would start their orientation course.

Dale Vernon looked around, waiting impatiently for his friend to show up. The late afternoon sun, still high on the horizon, made the ocean waters shine with silver reflections; the sand had been raked to offer an even surface for the upcoming game.

Dale rushed toward Conrad and yelled, "You're late!" Conrad responded with a blank look. "Wake up! We have to play volleyball— you know, the game where you toss the ball over a net?"

"Oh, that!"

Dale shot him a look of reproach. "You're wasting your time with that high-class broad. She's using you and you're too stupid to realize it."

Conrad shook his head. "Sonia is the sweetest thing on earth. You just don't like her, that's all." He grabbed the shirt Conrad had tossed him and slipped it on. "The usual team?" he asked.

"Yes. Yesterday we lost. Your replacement didn't work out." He scrutinized Conrad's body. "I hope you're in shape to play. We need to win so I can collect more than one thousand dollars in bets."

"I'm in great shape. The time I spend with Sonia energizes me." He winked at his friend.

"Puah! She's toying with you. She's a phony. I can smell it. And when you find out what her game is, it'll be too late."

"She's a kind woman, caught in a terrible situation. Her husband invested her money and lost it. On top of that, he's mean to her. I was in early one day and heard him calling her names just because she'd bought a new rug they couldn't afford."

Dale shrugged. "It's your business. I just can't figure out why she can be serious with you. You're nothing. You're an immigrant. Everybody hates immigrants, even if nobody admits it openly. Particularly Mexicans in this part of the country. They have no money and no social status."

"Ah, but you forget my physique." Conrad pushed his chest forward and bunched his forearms.

"Yeah, at any rate you're a macho man. But on any California beach there are a hundred young men looking like you, or better. And Sonia is so taken that she'll leave her husband and come to Canada with you? It's all BS."

A young man intruded, bouncing a ball from one hand to the other. "Ready to get creamed again?" he asked.

"Wait and see," Dale replied sharply. "Today our team is unbeatable."

In the courtyard of the shabby Bluewater Motel Conrad was barbecuing a few hot dogs when Dale came to sit close to him. "You played great. Your serve was a bullet fired just inside their baseline. No wonder we won 21 to 0." He tossed a bundle of bills at Conrad's feet. "Five hundred dollars, your share," he added curtly.

"I don't want it. I don't play for money and I'm against betting. You know that."

"Don't be an idiot. You need money to show off with that woman."

He cut a bun in two and extended it to Conrad. "Don't be cheap on relish and mustard."

Conrad complied. "You don't understand. She likes me for what I am. I don't have to do anything special for her."

Dale ate his bun in big bites. "You're barely nineteen. At your age you shouldn't get stuck on one woman. Do as I do. When I want to get laid, I sit alone in the middle of the beach. Sunset is *the time*. It's when women get into a romantic mood. It doesn't take long for a girl eager to please to come along." He laughed a strange, nervous laughter. "All I have to do is to be sure I don't catch a disease. No other worries. A different place every night. It avoids getting attached." He rose to slice another bun and dressed it. "I'm missing a few pickles," he said as he sat close to Conrad. "Yesterday you were away all day. What did you do?"

"Sonia, you know she's an interior decorator, right?"

"Yes. She probably sticks a few pins in some draperies and call herself an interior decorator."

Conrad ignored this remark and began eating his hot dog. When he spoke, his mouth was still full. "We went to a big house thirty miles from here, in the hills. I helped her hang the curtains." Conrad finished chewing. "You should see the place: high on a rise, with a quarter-mile-long driveway all in stamped concrete, at least thirty feet wide, flanked by cypresses. The house had a big hall with a cathedral ceiling. The drapes were fifteen feet long. Heavy. Sonia couldn't have hung them by herself."

"Why? She can't use a stepladder?"

"You're impossible. Are you jealous?"

"Not a fat chance. I want to make it in life. Big money, women, houses, boats, you name it."

"But then why do you want to become a policeman?" Conrad asked.

Dale shrugged. "I applied and got accepted. Nothing better to do at the moment." He paused. "And I like to be with you. Together, we can go places." He grabbed his bag and rose. "We'll move to another beach and another motel tomorrow. It isn't wise to hang around here much longer."

Conrad had not accepted Dale's money; he had, however, borrowed his best clothes, a pair of Levi jeans with matching shirt. He drove the Mustang to the Schneiders' house.

Just the idea of seeing Sonia Schneider excited his imagination and filled his senses. He wondered if she would make love to him right away or would first tantalize him with little games of withdrawal and rejection. Either way Conrad's anticipation for the encounter grew with every mile he drove.

Sonia was in the parlor, curved over a huge cardboard box; others were on the floor. She greeted him with a brief hello, wrapped a big terracotta amphora in layers of fine paper, set it down in the box, and sealed the box with tape. She then rose and gave him a peck on his lips.

Swiftly Conrad took her by the waist and drew her close. Her brown hair brushed his face and her subtle scent penetrated his nostrils. "I love you," he murmured. He only needed to look at her quick eyes and her sensuous mouth to feel aroused.

Sonia smiled at him but quickly pulled away. "Later," she said. "Now I have to pack. The truck will be here soon. You can help." She knelt beside an empty box, counted twelve pieces of cutlery, wrapped them together and set them in the box.

Conrad imitated her, even if at a slow pace.

When the box was full Sonia rose. She grabbed a colorful vase and a lamp shaped like a group of calla lilies stemming in different directions. "These are to be delivered to the shop directly. They're too delicate to be shipped."

"They're so beautiful," Conrad said. "They're almost transparent and yet the color comes through nice and clear."

"That's not all. Feel how smooth they are." She took Conrad's hand and rubbed it against the objects. "It's blown glass from Murano. Look how many shades! They're fragile, however. Fortunately I kept the boxes they were shipped in." Together they encased them between two lateral supports and slipped them into their containers.

"My husband always kept a couple of these lamps in his office here, at home. They were a great promotional pitch. Several clients wouldn't leave without taking one home. Too bad they have to go." She sighed.

"Where do they have to be delivered?"

"To the Collectors' Corner near the marina. They're expecting them."

"I know the shop," said Conrad. "I could take them there for you."

Sonia pasted a label on each box. "Tonight we're busy," she said, and shot him a seducing look. "But I'd appreciate if you'd do that sometime tomorrow. Set them in the garage for now?"

Sonia stood in the driveway, a worried look on her face as she watched a man loading her cargo onto the courier's truck.

"It's a sad story, my life." When the truck was gone, she turned to Conrad and caressed his bare arms. She leaned against him, her head on his chest. "The only thing that keeps me alive is knowing you love me," she said tenderly.

Conrad put his arms around her. "I'll take care of you. No need to worry." He rubbed his face against her cheek and kissed her. "Are you alone?" he asked.

"Yes. My husband is in Dallas closing up our shop there. Next week we'll close the shop in L.A. All our beautiful antiques will be gone."

"Sorry to hear that, Sonia." He kissed her again. "What can I do to cheer you up?"

"You can take me dancing, remember? At that place they just opened: The Moonlight." She ruffled his curly, dark hair. "I called and reserved a table. I also asked them to play our favorite song."

Conrad waited more than an hour for Sonia to get ready. Finally she appeared: a filmy dress whispered around her legs and her hair, arranged into short tresses at the front, fell softly over her ears. She linked arms with Conrad and together they walked over to Conrad's old Mustang. "I'm ready to enjoy our evening," she said winking at him.

They did not get tired of dancing, sitting only to have a drink or smoke a cigarette. Blue, red, and green beams cast from the ceiling created intermingling, colorful patterns on the dark floor.

Conrad wanted to spend a few moments alone with her, but every time he suggested they leave, she shook her head. At two o'clock in the morning, closing time, imitations of soft snowflakes invaded the dance floor.

Sonia put her arms on Conrad's shoulders. "It has been the most wonderful evening of my life," she murmured. "I'll remember it for ever. I love this music and I'm crazy about dancing."

While the closing song, *Spanish Eyes*, was being played, Conrad said, "I'd like to talk to you, Sonia. Let's go to a quiet place and discuss our future."

"Not tonight, Conrad. We'll have to find another time for that."

As the last notes resounded in the hall, Conrad slowly disengaged himself from her. "Then I'll take you home."

Conrad tossed in bed for hours before falling asleep. In the morning he was awakened by voices and splashing water. The new room at the Sunset Motel, where they had moved the day before, opened directly onto a pool area already filled with swimmers and sunbathers. He dressed, wondering what Dale had planned for the day. Dale was fun to be with; in the three weeks of their vacation he had organized different activities, from volleyball to surfing to whale watching. He would spend the entire day with Dale, since he was not going to see Sonia, in spite of her specific request, not today and not for a couple of days. He hoped a short separation would help clarify the situation. Her behavior had been somewhat consistent with Dale's suspicions—and Dale knew about women. He had put in his car the two items for the Collectors' Corner right after he had taken Sonia home; he would ask the shop to call her and let her know that the delivery had been made.

He found Dale in the motel coffee shop, intent on ordering breakfast. Conrad joined him.

"We're hired for a quick job," Dale said as he spread butter on his bun. "Your uncle, Gonzales the policeman, called. The station agreed to take us on one of their night tours as we requested, but, in exchange, we have to do them a favor."

"A favor? What kind?"

"Something simple. We have to take a trunk to San Felipe, across the border. They'll pay for the gas, and gives us fifty on top. Not a bad deal."

"Hmm...what's in the trunk?"

"Personal things belonging to a young officer who died two weeks ago. They have to go to his mother. He had no family here. They were looking for somebody who spoke Spanish and could say a few kind words to the woman. Maybe even spend a little time with her. I volunteered you for the job. We can pick up the trunk anytime today."

"Great. I have to make a delivery myself. In no time we'll be competing with the post office."

144

31

"No!" Lt. Detective Murray Stanton of the Silvaplana police station banged his fist on the desk. "You can't talk to your nephew. I don't want you intruding in this matter, you're family. You can watch through the one-way glass, but you can't be present."

"But the boy has nothing to do with the case," Ramon Gonzales retorted, his voice a high pitch. "He was here, at this very same station, Wednesday at 1:30 p.m. He crossed the Mexican border at 3:30 p.m. and stayed at the Vargo family house one full day." He stopped to inhale deeply. "He came through the same border this morning with his friend, and both came straight here to give us the gift from Vargo's mother. It has all been checked out. Conrad couldn't be involved even if he wanted."

Stanton put up his hand to stop Gonzales. "Enough. You can watch. You can't be there."

A small gift box lay open in front of Conrad and Dale. Set on red velour, a silver crucifix, finely chiseled, reflected light in all directions. "It's beautiful," Conrad said. "It was nice of Vargo's mother to express her gratitude to the police station in this way."

"Yes," said Dale. "But I have been staring at that cross for the last full hour. I'm getting sick of this place, fed up of waiting for what they want to tell us. When we arrived they sounded in such a hurry."

"Be patient," Conrad said. "Going to San Felipe has been an experience. Not pleasant, but...." He searched for a word. "Educational. It made me realize what the family of a policeman might have to go through."

The trip had hit Conrad hard. When Vargo's mother had heard that, during the shootout, her son's killer had died too, she had

145

looked at him sadly and said in Spanish, "So there is another mother or wife who grieves."

Death, grief, and murder—daily elements in a policeman's life.

Conrad had been proud of having been admitted to the Police College, since very few were selected every year, and, until today, he had been eager to start the training; now, however, he wondered if he was really fit for that kind of work.

With a shriek the door swung open and a giant of a man made his entry. "Lt. Detective Murray Stanton," he said bluntly. He briskly asked Dale to step outside and addressed Conrad. "Sorry to make you wait. But we need your help." He zeroed his eyes into Conrad's. "Claus Schneider has been murdered." He paused. "According to our sources, you know Mrs. Sonia Schneider. We'd like to know what kind of relationship you have with her."

Conrad lowered his eyes. "It's terrible," he mumbled. He did not speak for a long moment. Then, "We're friends," he said.

"How did you meet her?"

"She was stranded on the side of the road. That afternoon it was raining hard. I offered to change her tire. Afterward, she invited me to her place to dry my clothes and have a drink." Conrad stopped and looked down at his hands.

"The full story, Tormez," Stanton roared.

Conrad did not seem to hurry or be intimidated. "We met a dozen times. I helped her with chores in the backyard and around the house."

"When did you last see her at her place?"

"Tuesday afternoon I helped her pack, then we went out. I took her back around two o'clock in the morning."

Stanton leaned toward him. "Did you have an intimate relationship with her?"

Conrad blushed. "Yes, Sir." He finally met Stanton's eyes. "I'm afraid we fell in love."

"*We* fell in love? Do you think *she* fell for you?"

Conrad shrugged. "So she said. And I believed her."

A young officer entered the room and took Stanton aside. He murmured something into his ear.

"I'll be right there," Stanton told him. Turning toward Conrad he said, "You moved out of the Bluewater Motel, correct?" Conrad nodded. "Where are you staying now?"

"At the Sunset, a five-minute drive from here."

"Good. You can go now, but don't leave town. We want to talk to you again. Tomorrow."

Stanton closed the door behind him. "You said Mrs. Schneider went to Collectors' Corner on Wednesday afternoon? Let's go there and see what she wanted. All the moves she made that day are critical. They can tell us much more than all the depositions in the world."

"Another thing, Sir. Mrs. Schneider called Tormez at the Bluewater Motel a total of fifteen times in the last forty-eight hours."

"Interesting. I think I get the picture." He grinned. "Mrs. Schneider is a goner. Station a car outside the Sunset. We can't let Tormez leave. We need him to frame the woman."

Dale swiftly walked to the driver's side of Conrad's Mustang. "Move," he said curtly. "You aren't in any shape to drive."

"What kept you so long?"

"I went to see your uncle, Detective Constable Ramon Gonzales. He was eager to talk and I was eager to listen. I almost got the entire story behind the Schneider murder." He put the car in motion. "You have to be careful, Conrad. You can run into trouble. You're lucky your uncle is a nice man. He isn't chewed by the cancer of hurting people as most policemen are."

Conrad stared at the road ahead without uttering a word.

Dale continued, "I should tell you what I got. Claus Schneider dealt with antiques, some stolen, a few original, mostly fakes sold as originals. No paintings. A lot of Aztec, Chinese, Roman, and Etruscan artifacts, pots, and vases. Those kinds of things. His warehouse in Dallas was burned down. Arson. The insurance didn't pay. Four important museum pieces, stolen, were found in his L.A. shop. In short, Schneider was in trouble both financially and with the law. A year ago the Schneiders took out insurance, for one million dollars, on each other. That makes Sonia suspect number one." Dale stopped. "Are you okay?" he asked.

Conrad nodded and Dale continued, "Now your girl. It's true she had plenty of money when she married Claus. She inherited it from her previous husband who died of a heart attack while on a trip in Mongolia. Sonia was with him. Of course it was impossible to check out the circumstances of the first husband's death in detail. So some suspicion hangs over Sonia's head. Nobody denies that Claus had enemies but the murder took place in his home, with Sonia in and out of the house."

"How did Claus die?"

"A heavy object was swung over Mr. Schneider's neck from behind. It severed his neck. The man died between 2:00 and 3:00 p.m. on Wednesday. No fingerprints others than the wife's. She found him around 5:00 p.m. when she returned from shopping, she said, and called police." Dale parked the car close to the motel door. "They think the wife did it—it's a recurring pattern—but they have little to pin on her." Dale pulled on Conrad's arm. "Have you been listening or not?" he asked brusquely.

Conrad's voice seemed to come from the depths of night. "To every word you said. I was lucky to be away or I'd be a suspect too."

"You got the point. I'll try to find out what's in Sonia's deposition, tomorrow."

"You can't. It's impossible."

"Leave it up to me. I have my ways. You just be careful. The police may play games with you. And they won't be Sonia's kind."

32

Murder! Stretched on top of the bedspread Conrad watched the lights from passing cars flashing on the ceiling. Sonia was a suspect...could she have murdered her husband?

He remembered the first time she had made love to him. It was an experience he would never forget.

It happened in her parlor. It was beautifully furnished, with an all-black tiled floor, an ivory-colored chesterfield, and wall light fixtures that diffused a delicate glow. It was still raining hard outside when he slipped off his soaked shirt and gave it to Sonia to dry.

Sonia stood in the middle of the room. Her white shorts revealed long, nicely tanned legs; her top, tucked in the shorts, showed a slim waist and well-shaped breasts. She ambled toward him, her eyes engaging his.

Mesmerized and speechless, Conrad did not budge.

With her soft hands Sonia caressed his naked chest and kissed his nipples. Then she unzipped his jeans and pulled them down. She pushed him onto the soft leather chesterfield and knelt near him. The tip of her tongue ran over his lips over and over again. One after the other she took off her garments, each movement reminding Conrad of a cat on the hunt—slow and sly. She never uttered a word as she came to lie on top of him.

Her skin was smooth and lightly scented. Her hair brushed his body as she angled her head to kiss his earlobes, his throat, and, moving down, his chest.

Conrad felt lost but unable to stop her; his body was yearning more and more each moment. When Sonia tried to remove his underwear his hands promptly helped her.

Sonia kneaded his hips; she moved her hands down his legs, and said, "That's my boy, all muscles, so strong." She caressed his hardness, then took it in her mouth and sucked on it. Then, "I should stop here, because you want to taste some of me too, right?" She stretched up and moved beside him, her arms inviting him to come on top of her.

As Conrad shifted Sonia's slim body under his, his need for her reached a peak. He hesitated no more, and with one thrust he entered her. After that, all he could remember were her moans and cries of pleasure, mixed with his. They filled the entire parlor.

When he left late that night, his clothes were still wet.

Conrad sighed deeply. Never before had he thought love making could be so gentle yet so intense, and the memory of the passion he had experienced still sent sparks through his body.

Somebody was shaking him, but Conrad couldn't distinguish whether it was in his dream or real. "Let go, let go," he murmured.

"Wake up," Dale ordered with his metallic voice. He took Conrad by the shoulders and shook him hard. "I want to talk to you."

"What in the...." Conrad opened his eyes and stared at his friend. "Oh, it's you." He sat up, rubbed his eyes and focused on Dale. "I had a nightmare. Sonia's husband had been murdered." He only had to take a look at Dale to realize it had not been a dream.

Dale sat on Conrad's bed and took off the ID card pinned on his coat. "I went to the station, as I promised. You were right, the file with Sonia's deposition was kept in a safe. I couldn't put my hands on it, but I found out other important things."

Conrad took the ID card and looked at it. "LAPD? Where did you get this?"

"Oh, that. I've been collecting badges and ID cards since I was in grade school. They come in handy from time to time."

"But it has your picture on it!"

Dale grinned. "Of course, otherwise it wouldn't be useful." He took the card from Conrad's hands and stored it in his pocket. "I managed to stick around long enough to get two pieces of information. First, Sonia Schneider has denied having an affair with you. You were so taken with her that she felt sorry for you. That's why she hired you to do some work around the house. Second,

Wednesday she went to Collectors' Corner and tried to buy back the two items we had earlier delivered to the shop." Conrad listened carefully. "They were gone, however; sold to a Japanese customer."

Conrad became pensive. Nothing of what Sonia had done or said made any sense.

"You better get up and have something to eat. You look like you need a gallon of coffee, to start with."

"I'm going to call uncle Ramon," Conrad said after his third cup of coffee. "He'll tell me what to do."

"You uncle is out of town on a three-day mission. You're on your own."

Conrad nibbled at his danish. "What would you do in my shoes?"

"Don't volunteer any information. Don't display anger, no matter how upset you are." Dale finished his grilled cheese sandwich. "Your romance with Sonia? Make it sound casual, as though there was a lot of good sex and little affection. One may kill for love but seldom for sex alone." He quietly drank his coffee. "In reality the police have nothing to pin on you. But, if they think they can get what they need out of you, they will push hard, very hard. And be suspicious if they want to be your pal."

"Experience?"

Dale shifted his eyes away from Conrad's. "Some."

* * *

This time Stanton ushered him into a nicely furnished room. *A conference room,* Conrad mused instantly. With fuzz on the back of his hands and hair shooting out of his open shirt, Murray Stanton reminded him of a grizzly. When he moved he circled his arms around his big body, as though ready to catch a prey.

"So you're Gonzales' nephew," Stanton started, and gestured him to a chair. "And like your uncle you want to be a policeman. A Mountie?"

"No, Sir. Just an OPP officer."

"Too bad. The RCMP have a prestigious reputation." As Conrad did not react, he asked, "A Coke?" Conrad shook his head. "You see, Conrad, the department needs your help. We think you're a very nice man, caught in a situation your parents would definitely disapprove of."

Conrad stretched his arms on the table. He would have something to look at while Stanton was setting the bait. If only he would make it short....

"Murder is a terrible thing, you agree with me, Conrad?"

"Yes."

"Worse if the murderer has the trust of the victim. We can't betray those who trust us, right?" Stanton paused. "Are you at ease, Conrad?"

"So-so, Sir. I'd prefer to be on my way home to get ready for my training."

"At the Ontario Police College in Aylmer, right? It's still weeks away."

"Yes, Sir." Obviously his uncle had gotten the third degree. "But before that I have to attend an orientation session in Orillia." He hoped to express some sense of urgency so Stanton would let him leave, but Stanton waved off his statement.

"What we need is a few hours of your time to prepare you and an hour or so to do the job."

He was getting close. Conrad wondered if Stanton would butter him up a bit more. "I don't know if I can be of service, Sir." He probably could, but he doubted he would.

"That's the spirit! I like young people. Full of enthusiasm and ready to remedy the errors they've made."

Conrad brought his hands close to his mouth and looked at Stanton.

"I'll come to the point, Son. We suspect Mrs. Schneider committed the murder and we think she lied about the relationship with you, among other things. If we can prove that she did, we'll be entitled not to believe her on other important issues."

Stanton opened a Coke and began sipping it. "We believe she intended to frame you for her husband's murder. A young man in love can be pushed into doing foolish things, that's something a jury would be inclined to believe."

This time Conrad met Stanton's eyes straight on. "I would never be drawn into doing anything of that kind, Sir. Never."

"I know, I know. But you have to admit that, if we hadn't hired you for the Mexico mission, you could be a suspect, right?"

"I guess so." Going on vacation with the idea of living it up and ending up with an accusation of murder...that would have been something to remember!

"To find out the truth, I have an idea. You meet with Mrs. Schneider and ask her a few questions. Her answers could be very useful to our investigation."

It was out! He had to spy on her. Conrad wanted to know how far they would go to trap the woman into her own lies. "What kind of questions?"

"Why she said you two weren't lovers, why she called you at the Bluewater Motel fifteen times...."

Conrad lowered his eyes and pondered the situation. Sonia had lied, but what if she did so only to protect herself? Calling him was not a crime; she might have felt the need to talk to a friend.

Stanton continued. "We'll wire you, so that we can use her answers in court."

It was possible the woman had planned to kill her husband and kept him around to take the blame. But he was not the one who was going to find out. Sonia had declared she did not have feelings for him, and that set him free of any obligation toward her. She would have to go through rough times without him—*but to help frame her? It was out of his league.* When he spoke, he made sure his words came out low and grave. "I'd like to help your case, Sir, but, as you said yourself, betraying those who had put trust in you isn't a nice thing to do."

33

"Dale, why can't you go back to the station?" Conrad asked.

"The last time I was there I wore a police uniform and a false badge, and I talked to five or six people. I stuck around for more than an hour. There's a chance they'd recognize me. Those people are sharp, trained to observe what's going on." He shot Conrad a curious look. "What do you need, anyway? I thought our business in Silvaplana was finished, that we were ready to go home."

Conrad stopped packing his bag and sat on the bed. "I'd like to know what kind of object killed Mr. Schneider."

Dale pulled the cords of his backpack and tied them together. He kicked the backpack toward the door of the motel room. "Why?"

"Curiosity," Conrad replied.

The racket of an iron chair dragging on the cement floor made Conrad turn sharply. He had spent a quiet hour seated in the shade of a pepper tree, watching the children climb the slide and plunge into the water.

Stanton slumped in the chair, holding Dale by his arm. "Why did you send this jerk to the station?" He shook Dale by the arm. "He doesn't want to talk, but you will. You know something you didn't tell me."

Conrad sat up straight. "Let Dale go, please. Something popped up in my mind last night, Mr. Stanton. You have to believe me."

Stanton let go of Dale and pulled his chair very close to Conrad. He looked alert but at ease. "So why do you want to know what kind of object killed Mr. Schneider?"

Conrad closed his eyes. For a long moment he couldn't speak. His tongue was glued to his mouth and his heart felt like it was in a vise.

Finally he muttered, "Wednesday I took two boxes to the Collectors' Corner. One contained a big lamp set on a square base with sharp edges. The top was glass: three flowers opened widely to hold big bulbs. Their stems were made of coiled metal springs. These were flexible, but robust. The lamp was heavy, but could be easily grabbed and swung around using the springs." Blood rushed through Conrad's body; his heart throbbed. Making a big effort, he opened his eyes.

Horror was flashing through Stanton's face. The man had looked hard for evidence, and had been ready to play a ruthless game to get it, but he surely was not happy to have found it. Stanton was a hard-nosed cop, but still a human being disturbed by a vicious murder.

For a moment, the only sounds were the water splashing and the kids' excited voices. Stanton rose. "That's the kind of object we're interested in." He did not say it had been used to sever Mr. Schneider's neck. Obviously he was not supposed to. He stroked Conrad's shoulder. "You touched it, right?"

Conrad looked up to him. The knot in his throat did not allow him to talk. He just bobbed his head.

"Of course," Stanton said. "Let's go to the station. I know how hard it must be for you, Son. But we need you for a deposition."

On the way home Conrad kept quiet most of the time. The vacation had been full of excitement and adventure, and Dale had been a great companion—full of life, thinking of new activities all the time, and ready to try anything new. But he wondered…what was the reason Dale wanted to become a man of the law?

What kind of person was the real Dale Vernon?

* * *

"Dad! Dad!" Conrad couldn't open his eyes. As painful as the recollection of that thirty-one-year old vacation was, he did not want to let it slip away.

"Dad? Dad!" Bobo had joined in the noise but Conrad wanted to relive the ending.

Sonia had died of a stroke while awaiting trial. Conrad still remembered how he felt when he received that news: regret for a love that had not been, and relief that Sonia's destiny had been decided by the Almighty.

He took a deep breath. Now he could open his eyes and return to present time.

Isabel, dripping water all over, called him again. Bernice stood in front of him, puzzled. Bobo, taking advantage of his torpor, was licking his face.

"Dad, wake up!" Isabel repeated.

"You were dreaming. You kept repeating 'It's over,' " Bernice said with curiosity. "What's over?"

Conrad got a grip on himself and his surroundings. "Our vacation, of course. We have to pack. We're leaving tomorrow morning, remember?" He grabbed the pup under his arm and rose.

The sun had dipped into the ocean and taken, with it, the last memory of Sonia Schneider.

PART 5

34

Varlee, Ontario
January 2001

Back from his holiday, Conrad felt ten years younger. He had slept only a few hours but he was well rested and relaxed. The vacation in Jamaica had been a blessing, since he had been finally able to spend time with his family from dawn to dusk. He still had three free days before going back to work. It wasn't much, just a few hours to reorganize his house and make room for Bernice and Jerome. On Jerome's insistence, he decorated the walls along the staircases going to the second floor and into basement with the posters Jerome had collected over the years, mostly pop stars or solitary singers. With Bernice he approached a real estate agency for an estimate of Bernice's house. They both agreed to put it up for sale.

All together Conrad was pleased with the way things were going. Today he left home early to show Bernice's house to two potential buyers.

Jerome was removing the last few things from the house.

"Shit! Is it ever heavy!" Jerome kicked a big carton and made it land inside Conrad's kitchen. "Am I glad this is the last one!"

"Don't be so rough!" Bernice admonished him.

Jerome shrugged. With another powerful kick he tumbled the box down the stairs and into the basement. He had to trade the largest room in his mother's house for a small bedroom in Conrad's basement, and he would not be allowed to blast his music through the entire house. His mother's marriage had not been good for him. He took all his boxes into his new living quarters; he then unfolded a poster featuring Bon Jovi, and pasted it on the room's largest wall. He kept whistling *Misunderstood*.

He was soon hungry, so he strode back to the kitchen. He opened the fridge, made himself a three-deck sandwich and grabbed a Coke. He sat on a high stool and looked at his mother. He said, "You work more now than before. Why did you marry Conrad?"

Bernice kept chopping the vegetables she had lined up on the cutting board. "You don't understand, do you?" She put celery, tomatoes, and carrots into the pot that was already on the stove, and went to sit close to Jerome. She gently stroked his hand. "All the money I'll get from the house sale will be set aside for us, Jerome. For my retirement and for your education in case you want to go back to school."

"School, school! Why don't you buy me a car? I could move around and do things."

"What things would you like to do?"

Jerome turned his face away from his mother. "Some people asked me to work for them," he said.

"What kind of people?"

"I don't know...somebody who stopped at the garage where I work. They said they'd pay well."

At the noise of an approaching car Jerome rose briskly and grabbed his toolbox. "Have to go," he said curtly.

"Where to?"

"I don't know. The place is far away. They said they'd pick me up and here they are."

And he was gone.

A wonderful aroma drifted from the covered dish set in the middle of the table. Bernice lifted the lid and helped Conrad and Isabel to a warm stew. From a steaming pot she scooped mashed potatoes for both. Slowly, she poured a glass of white wine for herself.

"Not hungry?" Conrad asked. "This stew would resuscitate the dead. Pearl onions always give the meat a delicate taste."

Bernice stifled a sigh. "Jerome took off again. He said he was going to work on a house far from here." She looked at Conrad, a deep frown on her face. "Why do they have to work at night?"

Conrad helped himself to a bun and slathered it in butter. "Eat, dear, and don't worry. Tomorrow I'll stop by the shop where Jerome trains. I'll talk to the manager. I'm sure I can find out what's going on."

Jerome had returned in the middle of the night and slept until noon. When he entered the family room he had the shock of his life. "What are you doing?" Jerome screamed. With a big leap he neared Isabel and grabbed all the CDs she had in her lap. "Do you know how much these cost?" He waved them in from of her.

Instantly Junior, who was seated near his mother on the floor, emitted one long shriek, followed by many, short others.

Isabel took the infant in her arms, rose, and went to stand in a corner, her back to Jerome.

"You're totally demented!" Jerome howled. A peg in the middle of the room held two CDs; pieces of others were on the floor.

From the upper floor Bernice dashed to the family room. "What happened?" she asked.

"The demented bitch used my CDs to play horseshoes!" Jerome looked at the back of the records he held in his hands. "Totally ruined! She's destroyed six hundred dollars worth of music!" He stood in front of his mother, red in the face.

"You shouldn't have left them here…this is the place where Isabel and Junior spend most of the day."

"Sure, the fault is mine, now!" Jerome threw the CDs he had in his hands around the peg. "Done! This is not our place; this is your husband's home!"

"Jerome, please, let's talk it over in the kitchen. You're upsetting the baby!" Isabel was delicately bouncing Junior up and down in an attempt to calm him.

"No use talking! I'm getting out of here for good!" In big strides he reached the kitchen, then the basement.

Bernice patted Isabel on the shoulders. "Don't worry. Everything is going to be okay," she spelled out.

Isabel looked at her blankly and mumbled, "I'm sorry."

Bernice gave her a quick hug and walked into the kitchen, just in time to see Jerome leaving with a backpack.

It had taken Bernice a long hour to make Isabel feel at ease, but now, finally, mother and child were asleep. She sat at the dining table, close to Conrad. She had told him what had happened. "I'm worried about Jerome," Bernice said.

"Don't. I think I know where he is," Conrad said. "But let's leave him alone for the night. Tomorrow we should gather all the pieces of his discs, look at what they are, and buy him new ones."

Bernice nodded. "You said you might know where he's gone?"

"I think he's at the shop where he's doing his apprenticeship; he has friends there. I went to check up on him; the owner said he's doing well. You remember that fellow with the blue cab who came to pick him up? He's one of the owner's customers. He needed somebody to help him wire some fancy system in a house away from here. Jerome offered to do the work, since there was good money in it." As Bernice's frown did not leave her face, Conrad stroked her hand. "Cheer up, Bernice."

"I'm afraid he may turn out like his father...always upset, irascible, incapable of holding onto a job."

"Jerome is also your son, Bernice, don't forget it!" Conrad squeezed her hand. "Last week I saw him playing peek-a-boo with Junior. He was gentle as a lamb. Have faith, dear." He nibbled at the pork chop lying on his plate. "Our family is new. We all need time to adjust to each other."

35

Whistling, Conrad sat at his desk. He did not expect any big surprises. In his absence, the data relative to Operation Woman in Black had been entered into the computer. Later in the afternoon he would meet with the Crown prosecutor to prepare the case against Kurt Todd. *Time to clear my desk,* he thought, *of the stack of papers that had accumulated during the last few weeks.*

At noon he was satisfied—his desk looked neat. He opened his lunchbox with anticipation. He had seen Bernice and Isabel make that special Italian mayonnaise that could elevate the most modest sandwich to a gourmet dish. He could smell the mayo even through the Saran Wrap. He closed his eyes and bit into the rye bread. Nothing would prevent him from savoring his delicious sandwich made of roasted veal, tuna, and capers.

It was time to satisfy his curiosity and look at the face of the man who had outsmarted the police for a full five years. He downloaded Todd's file onto his PC. He was still cleaning the breadcrumbs from his mouth, when Todd's facial features took consistency on the screen.

Conrad's heart came to a halt. The man was no other than his old pal, Dale Vernon!

As before, when he had seen Al Garnett's photo, his mind replayed a scene from the past: that fatal day fifteen years ago he had learned Vernon was a corrupt policeman. That day Vernon stood before him, a gun pointing at him, not one single emotion on his face. With one shot Vernon had fired at his leg and severed their long-term friendship.

For the last fifteen years nobody had heard of Vernon, though the entire police corps was still hunting him. But the man had always been right under their nose, avoiding detection and defiantly practicing his criminal schemes. He had probably chosen his rocky headquarters close to Varlee just as a challenge to Conrad's presence. But finally Vernon, alias Todd, had been defeated, and he would not be able to count on anybody's mercy.

His spirits raised, Conrad got a sheet of paper, sharpened a pencil and outlined the order in which he would present to the Crown prosecutor the different crimes committed by Kurt Todd together with the evidence so far collected.

He was halfway through the list when Conrad vaguely heard somebody bounding up the steps of the station.

"Mr. Tormez?"

Conrad did not reply. Couldn't anybody function without him?

"Mr. Tormez!"

"Yes," Conrad howled back without lifting his head from the paper in front of him. "What's up?"

Finally he forced himself to look around.

Rudy Ashwald couldn't stop gasping. He walked around the desk and stood nearby, frozen, his face a blank.

Conrad gripped his arm and gave it a shake. "Talk!"

"Sir, it's Kurt Todd." The man's voice was rising, as if he couldn't believe his own words. "He's gone, Sir. He got away."

Conrad paled. "What the hell?" His chest tightened; his mind began racing. How on earth had Todd managed to slip away? That very same morning Todd was scheduled to be transferred to a maximum-security facility.

"You know the officer who took Todd in custody, Chris Vannini?" Rudy paused as if he was afraid to continue. "He had a heart attack. They're treating him at the hospital." The young constable inhaled deeply. "Todd escaped with his vehicle and his gun."

With one powerful jerk Conrad rose, sending his chair to land a few feet away. He gave orders as he descended to the main floor. "Keep it tight," he instructed his men. "Don't let him give you the slip. He's armed, so for God's sake, don't let your guard down. The man is dangerous—he's a crack shot!"

Kurt Todd had incredible luck. Vannini was young and strong, and nobody knew he had heart problems.

Back in his office Conrad began pacing, telling himself Todd did not stand a chance. They would get him. But the minutes dragged on without a single sighting. After an hour, Conrad knew in his heart they had lost him. Todd, like a modern-day Houdini, had slipped away.

Exhausted, Conrad plunked into his chair.

Now he would patiently wait to hear from the hospital about Vannini's condition. An hour crept away uneventful.

But then the news came.

He had lost to death one of his best men.

36

Todd knew he had to get rid of the GPS tracking device that was standard in all Varlee police vehicles. If not, he would be spotted immediately.

As the road began winding through the woods, he made a sharp turn into the forest and stopped. It took only a few minutes to strip the car of its spying device. He went back on the road, and drove for about twenty miles in the opposite direction. When a pickup truck with caged chickens appeared in front of him, Kurt Todd turned on the lights and signaled the truck to stop.

It was easy to subdue the driver; he was such an old man that he probably did not even know what was happening. Todd hid the cruiser in the woods, thinking it might be useful later.

Within three hours he was safe in his new house in the hills. He immediately took off the police uniform and went to check on Al Garnett, who was sound asleep on top of the bedspread with his boots on. Disgusting. The man had no sense of propriety. He grabbed the cellular hanging from Garnett's belt and moved into the kitchen. With a big chunk of cheese and a handful of crackers in his hands he sat to eat.

Something had gone totally wrong, he told himself. It was a miracle he had managed to escape.

He analyzed the situation. Al Garnett was too well known to the locals; Fred Kusteroff had been arrested as he entered his refuge; contacting any of his men could be dangerous except for Norman Arbib. Norman was a poor excuse for a criminal, but at the moment he was his only secure connection. He had been involved only in the surveillance of The Hermitage Resort Complex and in the stamp business. When Norman had been arrested because of the theft involving the Gronchi Rosa, the police had not found anything on him. They had to release him. So chances were his phone wasn't tapped.

"It's me," Kurt Todd said as Norman came to the phone. "As you know, they raided my refuge and got a lot of compromising material. I managed to escape. You must contact Clara at once. Find out what happened. Her last message said everything had gone well and she would deliver the tape. I tried to call her, but I got no answer." He paused. "Fred has been busted; probably many others, too. To be on the safe side I'm conducting all operations from the other site. You know where that is."

"Yes. Sorry to hear about Fred. He's such a nice guy."

What an idiot. The organization was in danger and Norman rationalized about personality traits. "Shut up. Contact Clara and tell her to be careful."

"Yes," said Norman at length. "Anything else?"

"News about the stamp?"

"I got a couple of names in Vienna. Nothing of substance."

Of course, he couldn't expect anything great from an idiot like Norman. "Get your ass moving!" he shouted. Better cut the conversation short since Norman had the knack of upsetting him. He gave him the number of Garnett's cellular. "Call me back as soon as you have news."

Norman Arbib roused himself and went out to a pay phone. He had hoped to walk away from this dangerous life, but Kurt Todd was free again, and he was the one who gave the orders. He had to give it to him: the man had luck with a capital L.

He placed a call to Clara Moffatt. The machine came on. Given the circumstances, he did not feel like leaving any messages. Better to drive to her place.

He parked his old Chevrolet a couple hundred feet away from Clara's condominium and unhurriedly walked to the building. He keyed in her apartment number and waited. No answer. He repeated the operation without success. He looked around. The place was fenced off, no way to sneak inside without being seen from the road.

He leisurely entered the main office. *Good,* Norman thought, when he realized that the manager was a woman. He always had it easy with women. "Got a promotion," he said with the tone of a bragger, "and wonder if I can finally afford a fancy place like this."

The woman smiled at him. "We have different prices, according to the number of bedrooms: one, two, or three. Depends also if you want a large dining area with a fireplace. Take a seat, please."

"Hmm…let's start with the two-bedroom and the fireplace. I plan to give parties, and a big room is what I need."

The manager read from a sheet, "Twenty-eight hundred dollars a month plus utilities." She waited for his reaction.

What do the people who live here do, Norman thought, *rob banks?* "That sounds reasonable," he said with a straight face. "May I see one?"

"I don't have any vacancies at the moment. But there's one that will become available next month. I can put you on the waiting list."

Norman rose, feigning disappointment. "It won't be necessary, if I can't see it," he said sternly.

"Wait, wait. We have a tenant who has been away for quite a while. On a trip, probably. I don't think she'll come back in the next fifteen minutes. I can let you in and look around."

"Your girl hasn't been seen in or out of her condo for the last five or six weeks," Norman reported to Todd. "There is no trace of Clara Moffatt."

"What? She came back after the tape had been made. She said so in a message left on her phone! She also said she had sent the tape!"

"Kurt, I asked at the convenience store on the corner, and checked with the garage attendant. They confirmed what the manager had said."

He only heard the word "Shit!" followed by a dry click.

Norman dialed Todd's number again. At the beginning he had not given much thought to the fact the woman who had been introduced to him as Savina Thompson resembled Clara Moffatt, but now…that could be of importance. "I wasn't finished," he said. He briefly reported about the encounter at The Hermitage.

"It can't be!" Todd said.

"I told you what I saw. That security guard at Garments for Pleasure reminded me immediately of Clara: she was about the same height, had similar body build, and same blond hair. And she was wearing a black dress."

In a subdued tone, unusual for him, Todd asked, "But then, what happened to my Clara?"

"Don't know, but I can find out."

Todd didn't speak for a few seconds. Then he said, "Go to Barrie. Her mother was in a nursing home for years. She died there. It shouldn't be difficult to find which one. They may be able to tell you when they saw Clara last."

"Consider it done." Norman paused. Maybe this was the time to save grace for losing the Gronchi Rosa. "What I found about this fake Clara, is it worth something?" He heard a mean laughter.

"Yes. I won't consider killing you any more," Todd said and rang off.

37

Varlee, Ontario

Nobody seemed to know where Savina and Denis had gone. Conrad had been trying to contact them since early in the morning, to no avail. Finally, around three o'clock in the afternoon, Denis answered the phone. Quickly, Conrad said, "I'm coming to see you. It's urgent. I'll be there in half an hour." He did not give Denis time to utter a word.

Savina stood in the hall, a soft white dress flattering her slim figure, her wavy hair once again framing her fine-featured face. She swiftly moved to greet Conrad.

"Thank you for seeing me." He took her hand and led her to one of the wicker chairs. He dragged another chair in front of her and sat in it.

Silently Denis joined them, a brief nod of his head acknowledging Conrad's presence.

"You look well," Conrad said to Savina. "We have to talk about Operation Woman in Black."

Denis interjected, "Cut it short, Conrad. There was a lengthy report on the capture of Todd and his men. We don't need any addition. Just spell out what trick you came here to play."

Conrad sighed. He deserved some hostility, but definitely not that much. "Bear with me, Denis, please. Todd has escaped. We were moving him to a high-security compound when the officer with him had a heart attack."

"You should have sent a man in good physical condition, not an old man close to retirement," Denis said sharply.

"Denis, shut up. Nobody could foresee a massive coronary occlusion in a man twenty-seven years of age, who had passed his physical with flying colors only two months ago." He paused. "He was my top man."

Savina finally spoke. "Sorry, Conrad."

Conrad took both of her hands. "Savina, I'm asking you to come with me. We can stash you away in some safe place. It'll be only for a short time, until we catch Todd. It won't take long now, since he has almost nobody to count on."

He turned toward Denis. "One week, maybe two."

"I don't see the point," Denis said. "Todd is on the run. He'll have no time to experiment with all that speech garbage you've been talking about."

Conrad stifled a sigh. "We got all the material Todd had accumulated, Denis. There are pictures of the two of you, with the date printed on them. Somebody took them, one of his men, I presume. Probably Kusteroff, since we found a ton of photographic material in his house. Todd is going to look for Clara. We've disclosed the record of her death, which, of course, was dated long before those pictures were taken." He looked straight into Savina's eyes. "I know the man. He is scientific, precise, up to date on the latest technology. It won't take him long to figure out what happened. He'll seek revenge. And he won't stop until he has you at his mercy. You aren't safe here, Savina. Kurt Todd has nothing to lose by hurting you. And he will, if you don't hide."

"I see," Denis said. "All right. We'll move somewhere else. But I don't want you around, Conrad. Not in my house, and not around Savina."

"Savina—" He had to make a plea. "You have my word I'll do my absolute best to protect you. Please come with me."

Savina looked at Denis then at Conrad. "We'll take care of ourselves," she said and rose. "But thank you for warning us of the danger." They both walked away.

Conrad stayed in his seat. He had been dismissed. Sad, very sad, since he cared a lot about Savina. *I tried my best*, he told himself. Operation Woman in Black was going to be costly, not only in term of money: the department had lost one of its finest men; he had lost Savina's and Denis' friendship, and his career was at stake. Conrad sighed and rose.

Now he had to take care of his own family since the meeting for Junior's custody was coming up next. He looked at his wristwatch; it was time to go since he was expected at the Court House in less than an hour.

The hearing took only fifteen minutes. As Conrad waited for the judge to make his decision on the temporary custody of Junior, Conrad reviewed the salient moments of his life. He had endured plenty of hardship, starting with Isabel's mysterious sickness. It was then that his life had taken a downturn. He relived the anguish of losing Isabel, the emotional difficulty of coping with her retardation, and the loss of his beloved wife, Sharon. And, when Isabel had disappeared, his life had almost lost any meaning for him—his house only an empty hostel. In the last few months his situation had drastically changed. He had gotten his daughter back, unharmed; he had gotten a squawky fellow that attracted everybody's love and attention; he had gotten a new companion who was cheerful and loving; he had gotten a stepson whom he might able to help and guide; and, with some luck, in a few weeks Bobo would be fully housetrained. He glanced at Bernice, who was seated beside him on an old wooden bench. It definitely felt good to be alive.

The chamber door swung wide open and Donald Stevenson, Conrad's lawyer, walked toward them, waving a piece of paper. "Done! From now on the two of you are in charge of Conrad Junior. The adoption will come later, but I don't foresee any complications."

Conrad and Bernice exchanged a look of relief, and rose.

"Congratulations. Not that I expected any problems, of course." Donald shook hands with both.

"Thank you," Conrad said, echoed by Bernice. "Don't forget the party: this coming Saturday at 6:00 p.m. we'll be celebrating the return of Isabel and the arrival of Junior in the family. We haven't done that, yet. You can bet on plenty of snacks and great cookies. Bernice bakes like nobody else."

"My wife and I will be there, Conrad. We wouldn't miss it for anything in the world. We are so happy you got your Isabel back."

Conrad stroked his friend's arm. "Can you give me a ride to the station? Bernice would like to pick up Isabel and Junior at the coffee shop downstairs and go shopping. I have to rush back. I have big problems at work."

A waitress was standing by a table, talking to Isabel. She turned around as soon as Bernice opened the door. Pointing at Junior she said, "He's a beautiful baby!" She then walked behind the counter and began making a new pot of coffee.

Bernice moved near to Isabel. "How is Junior?"

"Good. He drank his milk and went to sleep. Ready to go shopping?" Isabel rose and slipped her coat and woolen hat on, trapping some strands of hair under the coat's collar.

"Let me help you. You have beautiful hair. We want everybody to see it, right?" Bernice said, and spread Isabel's shiny hair over her shoulders.

Isabel nodded and, with a sudden movement, hugged Bernice so tight that Bernice couldn't breathe. When she finally let go, she said, "I love you." She then adjusted the scarf around the baby's neck. "Shopping! Junior needs booties and a top with a doggy on it." She pushed the buggy out of the coffee shop. "He needs diapers too," she said, and wrinkled her nose.

38

Todd was tired but couldn't sleep. He did not know on whom he could rely for a quick exit out of the country. Probably most of his men were under surveillance, those who hadn't been arrested, of course. He had lost all the sophisticated equipment and machinery that would allow him to create documents and contact people without being arrested. He had little chance to recover or replace them. All he had, hidden in the basement, was an arsenal, but even this was not complete. He had a good selection of guns but little ammunition; he had detonators but lacked time-delay devices. He had explosives but not enough to complete the small protective barrier he wanted to build around his tunnel. At the moment he couldn't do anything and he couldn't move.

Distraught, he turned on his satellite TV and tuned into one of the Toronto channels.

Conrad Tormez took up most of the screen, his powerful voice shouting into the microphone. He assured all viewers that Kurt Todd, alias Dale Vernon, did not have a chance, just a few hours of freedom before being captured again. *Disgusting*, Todd thought. He should find a way to get to him, and shut him up—permanently if possible.

He had just stretched out in a chair when Norman called.

"Kurt, I was in Barrie. I found the nursing home where Clara's mother spent her last three years. The management never saw Clara when her mother passed away. From what they can remember, the funeral was arranged by an out-of-town relative. Nobody could tell me anything about Clara."

Todd's heart crunched. Clara had disappeared and the police had replaced her with somebody else. But what did they do with his girl? His voice was hoarse when he said, "Check the list of deceased people in Varlee. And don't call me back until you find what happened to Clara."

The sun had disappeared behind the rock at the back of Todd's house. Wearing dark green coveralls and yellow helmets, Kurt Todd and Al Garnett got in the pickup and began driving. The snow's top layer, melted during the warmest hours of the day, had formed a thin crust of ice which made the tires squeak on impact.

"Finally we get out here! Can we go to Tim Horton?" Garnett asked.

"No. We're out for business. To get the police car I left near the branch off Road 62. I need it for my next operation. This pickup is hot. We have to ditch it. Then we come back here."

"What are we going to do? We can't hide in this damned place forever. Shit! It's in the middle of nowhere!"

Kurt did not answer right away. "I have a plan, but I need to do some checking before I take action."

Garnett paused, uncertain. "I have something on Tormez. We could use it to dig our way out of trouble."

A stack of plastic containers, shaped and painted to look like logs, occupied one corner of Todd's basement. Seated on a stool, Todd took one of the look-alike logs and filled it with pellets of PETN. After Al Garnett had repeated his story, Kurt said, "Let's recap. Isabel's real baby, your baby, died and you buried him close to the log house." Al nodded. "Are you telling me that Isabel Tormez' baby is not her baby?" Todd deposited the container he had just filled in a box and picked up an empty one.

"Right. I think that baby is the Simpsons' baby. You remember the people who died in the plane crash? Their child was never found."

Todd's hands moved nervously, shoving in one pellet after another into the container. "Interesting."

"You remember how much time Conrad used to spend with Isabel, trying to make her talk properly, to make her toss a ball back to him, to help her with her arm movements?" Todd looked at him and nodded. "He's a born father. He's probably very much attached to this baby. We could blackmail him." Al Garnett opened his mouth in a smile, weird, since his two front teeth were missing.

Todd threw the second container into the box. He rose and began pacing the basement. "Let's put two and two together. Tormez has taken advantage of the fact that I never communicate directly with Clara when an operation is on the go. We just leave messages for one another. Always on her machine." He stopped and stood in front of Garnett. "On the Internet I discovered a system that allows a person to speak as somebody else. I think Tormez made use of it. What he's done with Clara, I don't know. He replaced her with somebody else, and disguised her voice to make me believe it was Clara's. He's set up an elaborate snare to get at me."

"Do you think he killed her?"

"Nah. Thrown in jail or in some hospital."

"Let's make him pay. Make him drop the charges against us in exchange for our silence."

Todd shook his head. "Tormez can't do that. Not legally and not in the open. But he could let us slip out of the country, in exchange for not blowing the whistle on Isabel's baby."

Al Garnett clapped his hands. "Then, when we're safe, we blackmail him again...."

Todd threw his head back and laughed. "I see you've learned, working for me."

The phone intruded with its piercing sound. Todd turned the cellular on. "Yes?" It was Norman Arbib. Todd did not utter a sound; he just listened for a few seconds. Then slowly he switched the cellular off and neared the empty wood-like containers. With all his might he kicked one container after the other and sent them smashing against the wall on the opposite side of the basement.

Al Garnett looked at him questionably. Everybody knew it was dangerous to talk to him when he was upset. And now he was furious. But Garnett was entitled to know what was going on since he was part of his team. "Clara is dead. She had a road accident on her way to Barrie, two months ago." He crossed his fingers and twisted them so hard that his knuckles shrieked. "Tormez has replaced her with somebody else, and set up a trap to get us all." He paused. "But he failed, and now he has to pay." He paused. *"Will I ever make him pay!"*

* * *

176

"So what?" Conrad shouted into the mouthpiece as he pushed on the button that would automatically initiate tracing the incoming call. "Let's say you come out to proclaim that Isabel's baby is the Simpsons' missing child. Then what? Does it make any difference?" He paused to let Al Garnett understand he did not have any arrows in his bow. "The Simpsons were flat broke. When the accident happened they were on their way to visit the only family they had: Mrs. Simpson's seventy-five-year-old uncle! He had no money either. Now, I can guess where you buried your baby. In the ground on the right side on the cabin. I saw a cross near the log house!" He paused again before hitting Al Garnett with his last, most powerful argument. "But once the corpse of what you call your baby is exhumed and analyzed, you'll be charged with rape and abduction of a thirteen-year-old girl, plus cadaver occultation." Conrad laughed as loud as he could. "But of course ten years more or less will make no difference to somebody who'll get life!"

A click on the end of the line told him Al Garnett had been quickly convinced to leave things alone. He waited about ten minutes to give the computerized system time to analyze the data just acquired. Then he looked at the monitor of his PC. Al Garnett had placed the call from about two hundred miles away, using a stolen cellular. Even if he got in contact with the OPP and dispatched a cruiser, Garnett was too experienced to be caught on the spot. But there was one thing Garnett could do: he could go to Barnist and remove the remains of his dead son. Then Garnett would have something to blackmail him with.

Conrad drummed his fingers on the desk, searching for inspiration. Finally it came to him. A cellular phone hidden on top of the cabin door, coupled with a sound amplifier, would detect the presence of an intruder—that is, if there was a tower close enough to the log house to pick up the signal. To find out, he should get in contact with the phone company serving the region and with the local police station.

* * *

Near Barnist, the Rockies

Ron Donavan stopped his car in front of the log house that had been Isabel's home for more than a year. The door had collapsed, letting snow drift inside. With two big steps Donavan walked over the snow ridge and deposited two cardboard boxes that contained food, cleaning products, and other everyday necessities—his big shopping before going into seclusion. Unexpectedly, the trip from Toronto had lasted ten full days as the wind kept whipping the prairies and a snowstorm had forced the closing of the Trans-Canada Highway. In the few nights he had lodged in a motel, he had learned of Kurt Todd's escape. He had not dared to contact him to ask if his name was among those that had fallen into the authorities' hands. He had concluded that it was better to play it safe and keep a low profile, at least for a few weeks. Tomorrow he would meet with his mother on the outskirts of Calgary. She would bring him the ten thousand dollars he had asked her to cash for him. With that money he would survive until he found a suitable place to relocate.

Donavan got busy. He cleared the fireplace of old ashes and stacked up the kindling to build a fire. As the first flames leaped up, he dropped two logs on top. He made sure that the Coleman lamp contained enough fuel for the next few days and cleared out all the snow accumulated inside. Armed with a hammer, a few nails, and some plywood, he decided to repair the door. But before going to work, he needed to break the feeling of desertion that the place exuded. He switched on the little radio he had with him. To his surprise, the reception was excellent.

39

In the backseat of a GMC Aurora, Savina clung to Denis and stroked his arm. Day after day she had hoped to hear of Kurt Todd's recapture; instead weeks dragged on without even the smallest hint about his whereabouts. Fred Kusteroff, and the men arrested as a consequence of the raid carried out in Todd's headquarters, hadn't provided the authorities with any useful information. Conrad had once more advised her to accept police protection. He knew the man well, he had told her; he was capable of anything. If Todd discovered that Savina had camouflaged herself as Clara and set the trap that had led to his arrest, he would put her on the top of his avenge list. Savina had again refused to go into hiding and stayed in the Taillards country house, carefully avoiding meeting with strangers.

Denis patted her hand. "Don't worry, sweetheart," he said. "Everything is going to be fine." Together they had decided to break Savina's seclusion and spend a day at Niagara Falls. Mingling with the incessant flow of tourists would provide a good cover.

They were heading toward Highway 403 when a cruiser signaled them to pull over.

"Why did they stop us? We weren't speeding. Did you renew the car license?" Denis asked Charles Smith, his old chauffeur.

"Yes, Mr. Taillard. All the documents are in order. Mine too. I checked them before we left."

The cruiser stopped right behind their car. A tall man, wearing a dark helmet with a dark visor, waited patiently for Charles to lower the front window. "Step out, please," he said curtly.

Charles was just out of the car when the policeman threw him onto the ground, kicked him, and shouted a few orders to him. Charles quickly moved a few feet away. Through the open window Todd pointed a gun at Savina and Denis. "Get out. Now!" he shouted.

As neither Savina nor Denis moved, Todd opened the rear door and pulled Savina out. Denis, meanwhile, opened the door on his side and jumped out.

Todd did not lose any time. He pointed a gun at Savina's head and shouted, "If you take another step, I'll shoot her."

Savina dragged her heels in the ground and kicked Todd's legs until Todd smacked her head with his gun. Senseless, Savina fell to the ground.

Denis stood motionless between the car and the cruiser while Todd walked to the opposite side. Todd opened the rear door, pushed Denis inside, and hit him over the head. He loaded Savina's inert body into the passenger side and entered the cruiser.

He began driving, knowing he would have a quiet ride on the way to the arranged rendezvous.

* * *

Varlee, Ontario

Five weeks had passed since Todd's escape. Three more men had been arrested, bringing to six the number of people charged with affiliation to Todd's criminal ring. Conrad, however, was not an inch closer to capturing Kurt Todd than he was right after his escape.

He was pondering his bad luck when Constable Rudy Ashwald walked into his office. Rudy had just graduated from the police college in Aylmer. He was knowledgeable and eager to please. When he was around Conrad, he always looked for extra work. The men at the station had immediately taken advantage of his personality. If there was bad news to be announced, they would send Rudy. After six months, the poor guy had still not realized what was going on. His appearance in Conrad's office meant trouble on the horizon.

"Yes," Conrad said.

"There's a man outside. He wants to talk to you. He's all bruised but doesn't want to be taken to the hospital. He's blathering about some kidnapping."

"Send him in," Conrad said. His chest tightened, his stomach churned. Something to do with Kurt Todd, he could feel it. He gave a look at the man as he entered and slumped in the chair reserved for visitors. "Bring in a glass of water," Conrad said to Rudy.

Between one gasp and the next the man said, "My name is Charles Smith. I'm Mr. Taillard's chauffeur." He eagerly drank from the glass Rudy had deposited in front of him. "I was taking Mr. Taillard and his companion to Niagara Falls, when we were stopped by what looked like a patrol car." He assumed a contrite look. "The policeman threw me on the ground and pointed a gun at Mr. Taillard and Ms. Thompson. He ordered them out of the car." In one big gulp, he finished the water.

"The description of the man?" Conrad asked, although he already knew the answer.

"Tall. Skinny. Blue eyes."

Conrad sighed. What he feared might occur had. He took a map out of his drawer and unfolded it before Mr. Smith. "Please tell me where it all happened."

The chauffeur took his eyeglasses out of a hard container and slipped them on. He pointed at a spot on the map and said, "He told me to get in contact with you and tell you that he'll keep the girl around for a while." Smith stopped, uncertain. "But he'll kill Mr. Taillard, since you—" The man stopped again.

"Another glass of water, Rudy," Conrad ordered. Then he turned to Mr. Smith. "I understand how hard it must be for you, Mr. Smith, but you have to tell me everything, otherwise I can't help Mr. Taillard."

"Since you messed with his girl," the man whispered.

Conrad shrugged. "Anything else?" Smith hesitated again, clearly in pain. Conrad couldn't decide if it was physical or emotional.

"He took the keys to my car. I walked toward town and got a ride." He paused and looked at Conrad, worry all over his face. "I came here right away."

"Thank you, Mr. Smith. We'll take you to emergency. It's better if they check you out. Don't worry about Mr. Taillard's car. We'll take care of it."

Conrad wondered if he could send Rudy Ashwald to break the bad news to his boss. For a moment, he sympathized with that strategy. He looked at his wristwatch. It was 12:30 p.m. His boss was out for lunch.

He had time to think.

* * *

A truck was parked halfway up the trail. Its top, at the back, was nothing but a twisted metal frame covered by a worn-out, discolored canvas. Kurt Todd maneuvered his cruiser close to the back of the truck and killed the engine.

Al Garnett pasted a sticker on the license plate and turned around to face Todd. "Hi," he said. "All done."

"Come give me a hand with my two prisoners and get a few feet of rope. I had to smack them over the head to keep them quiet." He opened the police car doors.

Garnett rose from his kneeled position and neared Todd. "What do you think of my work? Good, eh?" He opened his mouth in a big smile. "Stole the truck from a farm one hundred miles from here; got a license plate from a junk yard and pasted the fake sticker on the plate—all this," he looked at his watch, "in less than two hours!" Pride seeped from his mouth. "And that's not all. I got boxes and branches to make the truck look full. That's what you ordered, eh?"

Do people have to be praised for doing their jobs? Todd curtly bobbed his head. He lifted Savina from the passenger seat and over his shoulder and deposited her in the truck.

With some effort, Garnett did the same with Denis. He threw a rope around the prisoners' chests and fastened it to the metal frame. He tied Denis' wrists together. He then quickly jumped out and joined Todd in the driver's cab. "Everything okay?" Garnett asked.

"No problem whatsoever," Todd replied.

Garnett rubbed his hands together. "When do we kidnap Isabel Tormez? I'd like to have a girl too," he said. "We leave the stupid baby with Conrad. It was good when the kid wasn't around."

Todd gave him a cold look and examined the devices on the dashboard. "You idiot! You forgot to get gas!" he shouted. "You know we can't stop at a pump with this kind of load!"

"Shit! I forgot! There's a container at the back. It's empty, but I can walk to a pump and fill it up." He jumped out of the cab and quickly returned waving a red canister. "Be back in a minute. I saw a gas station half a mile from here." In big strides Garnett disappeared from sight.

* * *

Conrad drove home, exhausted and frustrated. He had not gotten any new information out of any of Todd's men. They appeared to be small fish who worked on specific jobs Todd ordered them to do, here and there, and from time to time. At the moment he wasn't interested in gathering evidence against them as much as eliciting information on Todd himself, his whereabouts, his habits, and anything that would lead to his arrest. He had spent a full hour with Fred Kusteroff; on the advice of the Crown prosecutor he had offered immunity in exchange for Fred's testimony on Todd's criminal activities. He had the feeling Kusteroff knew a lot about his boss. But the man refused to open his mouth; his lawyer informed Conrad he had nothing to say.

From the papers the police had found in Todd's hideout, Ron Donavan emerged as a key man in Todd's organization. They had swooped on his farm the night they had arrested Todd. They found incriminating material, but no sign of the man. Out of the country? If so, he had probably found out about his boss's arrest and chosen to stay away. Too bad, since Donavan was clearly in much more trouble than Kusteroff. This would make him a better candidate to accept a reduction of charges in exchange for information leading to Todd's arrest.

Things being the way they were, he'd better think about how to rescue Savina and Denis directly, without counting on Todd's men. There wasn't much time left, and they were both very dear to him. Savina was almost a daughter to him and Denis was the son of his parents' lifetime employer, Mr. Jacques Taillard. When the Taillard family had moved to Varlee, Jacques, recently widowed, had looked for a couple who could take care of his household and sports club. Conrad's mother had helped raise Denis and Veronica while his father had taken care of the maintenance and repairs of both the family residence and the Varlee Country Club. Conrad still remembered the little house on Taillard land where his parents had lived for more than thirty years.

Yes, he should think of Savina and Denis, now in the hands of a maniac who would not hesitate to harm them. The spot where they had been abducted was only one hundred and twenty miles from Varlee, indicating that Todd was well within reach. *For how long?* Conrad asked himself. *Would Todd try to leave the country?* If so, he would keep Savina and Denis alive until he was out of trouble. Maybe he would leave them in a place with some clues to follow as a way to sidetrack him, since Todd knew that the police would concentrate on freeing the hostages before trying to capture him. In this case Savina and Denis would be safe.

If he could only guess the way Todd planned to take off...with the Ontario police and the airports alerted, would Todd's try to take off by water? Hmm...unlikely, since big portions of the surrounding lakes were frozen solid. In any case Todd's little secluded harbor was under surveillance.

But what if the threat reported by Denis' chauffeur was for real? Since he was dealing with Kurt Todd, he should also think of the absolute worst case—certain death for Denis and harm, if not death, for Savina.

Conrad drummed his fingers on the desk. The situation was dramatic.

40

The truck bounced hard at each bump—and the side road was nothing but one bump after another. Denis, recovered from the blow to his head, became fully awake. He wriggled close to Savina and called her name.

Savina opened her eyes. "Where am I?"

"In a truck. We've been kidnapped," Denis said in an undertone. 'We're tied together and to the truck: feet and feet of rope, not too tight, that's good. The problem is that it's pitch dark. I can only get my bearings using my fingers. And, shit! my fingers are cold and my wrists are tied together. It might take me some time to shake the rope off."

"I'm freezing," Savina murmured.

With his feet Denis retrieved Savina's coat, lying a few feet away, and threw it on top of her.

"Oh, now I remember: the police car. It was Todd, right?"

"Yes. I think it was him, unfortunately."

"Do you think Todd will kill us?"

Denis sighed. "Things don't look bright. Conrad said the man was dangerous, and that he'd be looking for revenge. When he pointed the gun at us, in the car, I looked at his eyes—they kept shifting. He blinked nonstop. Even his eyebrows couldn't stay still."

Denis was busy feeling the rope around his waist, trying to push it down his legs. "Since we're tied together, we may have a problem. When I get my rope loose, I might pull on yours, making it too tight. Scream if I do!"

"Yes, I'll, but it's okay so far." For a while neither spoke, then Savina said, "The man is dangerous and unpredictable. That was Conrad's warning." Her voice was a mere whisper. "I should have listened to him. Conrad has a ton of experience—I've seen him at work guessing at a criminal's next move, predicting what would happen in a week, then a year from now."

"Sorry I didn't go along with his suggestion. Will you forgive me?"

"Oh Denis, there's nothing to forgive. We decided together. Do you think Conrad will come to our rescue?"

"What hope do we have? He doesn't know where we are, even if Charles went to the police—if Todd didn't kill him, I mean. I don't know where we are either. Did we stop on our way here? I don't even know how far we are from where we were kidnapped. I was out until a short while ago, when the corner of the tarp got loose and lashed at my face."

"I heard Todd telling Charles to contact him. Conrad can figure out a lot of things, connections. He should be able to guess in which nook of the country we are. Did you see any signs? Houses? Gas stations?"

Denis shook his head. "Todd is following secondary roads. The one we are now on is just a trail cutting through the bush. We might be in the middle of nowhere. But we must have driven some miles, since it's two o'clock in the morning."

"How do you know?"

"My watch's hands become luminous in the dark."

Savina became fully alert. "I'm wiggling among the loops of the rope on my side. Then I can sneak out from underneath. A couple more loops and I'm free, I think. How are you coming with yours?"

"I thought I got rid of all the rope, but now it's wrapped around my ankles. I need to step out of them. Then we can jump off. At the next turn, when this old truck is forced to slow down. We can't miss, since this trail is full of bends and turns." Denis kept maneuvering among the several loops. "Done!" he screamed. "I even got my hands free. Now I'm ready for action!"

"Me too!"

At that moment the truck took the next turn at sustained speed, propelling Savina and Denis against the opposite side of the truck.

"Ouch!" Savina yelled. "My poor head!"

"Shit, now that we were ready to jump!"

The truck began to hobble uphill. The driver shifted one gear down then another. When he reached a small clearing he turned off the engine.

The old truck had stopped in front of Todd's garage. Garnett stepped out and cleared the garage of old boxes, of the skidoo, and of a workbench, to make room for the clunker. Todd drove inside carefully so as to not brush against the walls.

Just recovered from being tossed around, Denis and Savina jumped off the truck. They had only made it outside when Todd and Garnett reached from behind and threw them onto the cement floor. "And where did you think you were going?" Todd asked.

There was no reply.

"What do we do with them?" Garnett asked.

"Put some tape on their mouths to start with. Then take the Taillard boy to the living room and tie him to a chair. I'll take care of the woman." Todd grabbed Savina by the waist and dragged her into the house—Savina kicking all the way.

Todd's bedroom, on the upper level, was sparsely furnished. In a nook close to the window were a small table and a chair; in the middle, a king-sized bed with a footboard and headboard. One 15-Watt light bulb hung from the ceiling, giving the place a spectral atmosphere.

Savina added the use of fists to that of her feet, but Todd had no problem keeping her at a convenient distance, kicking her to push her ahead of him. He pulled off her coat and handcuffed her. "It'd be wiser to stop fighting. You'll only make things worse for yourself." He threw her onto the bed as though she was a sack of potatoes and sat close to her. "So you wanted to play Clara, eh? Let me see how well you play her favorite role—fucking." He threw his head back and laughed, then he ripped off her dress. He tossed the pieces away. "In your phone message you said you'd made a tape. You must have practiced a lot with your friend. Is he a good fuck?" He paused. "I forgot you can't talk with that big piece of duct tape on your mouth. But that's the way I like a woman—quiet." From his pocket he extracted a knife and cut her bra with a decisive gesture; he slid the blade down until it met with her underwear. "My hand isn't too firm these days. All due to that friend of yours, Conrad Tormez." He moved his knife up to her throat and slid it down again, this time scraping her skin. "I could leave you with some scars, you know, and you wouldn't like them, eh?" Savina closed her eyes. "Open those eyes! I want to see pain in them. I want to see terror about what will

187

come next!" Savina opened them, tears flowing down her cheeks. "I want to see you shake and sweat. It gives me pleasure, and you want to give me pleasure, right?" Todd touched the elastic band of her tiny slip. "Cheap underwear you have on, girl, not like Clara. This elastic band is very tight." He lifted up high and suddenly released it; when the band left its red mark, he did it again, and again. Savina blinked and shook, her stomach red. "Enough playing," he said brusquely. "Let's get down to business." He cut her slip in the middle and opened her legs. "I won't cut you there. Not yet, I mean," he said. He fastened each of her ankles to the footboard and unzipped his pants.

Noise from the main floor stopped him cold. There was a scream, then another, then the sound of crashing objects. Todd swiftly rose. "Don't move," he said to Savina, and laughed at his own joke. He strode out of the bedroom and locked it. He quickly went downstairs and opened the living room door. "What the hell…." Al Garnett was on the floor, holding his groin. "Where is Taillard?" Todd asked without paying attention to Garnett.

"Don't know," Garnett said and moaned. "I'm hurt."

Garnett was a giant of a man yet cried like a baby, hoping to attract attention. *Disgusting*, Todd thought. "I want to know what happened. And, if you don't stand up, I'll kick you more."

Garnett turned on his side and slowly rose. "He had a knife. He waited until I bent to tie his ankles to the chair, then he stabbed me in the arm. I'm bleeding!" he said and stretched his arm under Todd's face.

"It's a superficial cut. You were lucky." Todd looked around. It was dawn now and light sifted through the bare windows. "He can't have gone too far. Let's go after him."

"But I'm hurt," Garnett pleaded.

"You have always been injured. In the head, since you were born!" Todd walked out of the room and came back with a towel. He cut a strip out of it and wrapped it around Garnett's arm. "Now, let's go to find Taillard. Then I'll send you for an easy drive. I need some stuff from Donavan's farm."

Left alone in Todd's room, Savina shifted her body around helplessly. She couldn't scream—assuming that screaming could help—and couldn't use her hands or legs.

Feeling powerless and very vulnerable, she exploded into tears.

Todd pushed Garnett out of the door, down the corridor, and into the garage. From one of the shelves he grabbed a flashlight and walked outside, swaying the light left and right. "Found it!" he shouted. "I can see some tracks. He took the skidoo. Since we didn't hear it, he must have dragged it some distance." He took a few steps following the ridges left by the vehicle belt. "The man is still on foot. He couldn't have gone too far. We'll get him." He turned toward Garnett.

He was standing on the threshold of the garage, his hand on his groin. "I can't walk," he blabbered.

"I know, I know, but you can drive. Go to Donavan's place and get a box of Semtex. Ron keeps it in the shack in a barrel labeled *Corn Seeds*." He gave Garnett the truck keys. "Read the label. Don't come back with something else as you did last time!"

"*Semtex*! Why do you need more of that stuff in the house?" Garnett's voice was querulous. "You already have enough to blow up house, garage, *the works*!"

"It's not for the house. It's for the tunnel."

"But the tunnel is finished: it's all nice and clear."

Todd spelled out his words. "I need it to fill more of those logs in front of the tunnel, idiot! You can't understand. Move, do as you're told." He pushed Garnett toward the truck. "Pick up the electrician. There's still equipment to be hooked up, and come back right away." A headache was spreading from the back of his head toward his temples. He needed sleep. "Leave the cellular on. If you're followed or the police pull you over, give me a shout. It's important."

Reluctantly Garnett left.

He should go get some aspirin, but first he had to catch Taillard.

Todd turned off the flashlight, since now there was enough light to easily spot the tracks left by the skidoo. He crossed the clearing at the side of the house and scrutinized the few bushes and the big clumps of grass lying ahead. He spotted the silhouettes of a man and a vehicle and heard the starter. The skidoo did not budge. Todd got his gun out of the holster and quickened his steps toward Denis Taillard. When he got within shooting range he shouted, "Freeze or I'll shoot!" As Denis complied, he ran toward him and handcuffed him. "I'd like to kill you now, but you may be useful to me, for a while

189

yet." He kicked him and pushed him toward the house. "Inside," he ordered. His headache was reaching gigantic proportions. It was a migraine; he needed quiet and darkness. As he was tying Denis to a chair, colorful patterns started to obscure his vision, and they became more vivid and more frequent. He slumped on the nearby chesterfield and covered his eyes with his hand—he needed a few minutes of rest.

Todd jerked his head and looked at his chest, where his cellular was blinking and ringing. He grabbed the phone and turned it on. Garnett's grouchy voice sounded miles and miles away. "They stopped us, Kurt. The police: they have guns pointed at us...."

In the background Todd could hear the usual rites of the arrest. "Shut off the cellular!" he yelled, and waited for a click that did not come. Both his and Garnett's phone were stolen, but the haul between the two last towers would pinpoint Todd's approximate location. *Things were getting bad, real bad.* Garnett had been a liability since the beginning. He had hired him only because of the lucrative business Garnett's father provided him with. He should have got rid of him a long time ago. Because now...now he knew what was going to happen: the police would try to cut a deal with Garnett. The authorities had ample time to study Garnett's personality and adapt to it some of their canny strategies. Under the circumstances, Garnett would give his old boss away; maybe not today, not tomorrow, but surely in the near future.

He had to face reality. He was alone against all and everything. There was only one thing left to do: to engage Conrad in an ultimate challenge.

41

From the far end of the corridor Conrad couldn't distinguish the features of the two men just arrested. One kept his head down. As Conrad walked toward them, his heart skipped a beat. "Jerome?" The young man did not answer, his eyes stuck to the floor. "It can't be!" Conrad said.

"Jerome Berstow, age seventeen. No previous arrests, from what we know so far." Constable Rudy Ashwald had spoken. "The other man is Al Garnett, wanted on two counts of fraud and for carrying a gun without a permit. We caught them driving a stolen vehicle and transporting something that looks like Semtex. The lab is checking." He glanced at the pad in his hands. "There was also a stolen cellular phone in the truck."

"Oh, I see, an old acquaintance!" Conrad gave Al Garnett only a glance; he would take care of him later. He stared at Jerome for a long moment. "You weren't in good company," he said bitterly. As Jerome lifted his eyes, Conrad gave him a look of reprimand. "I'll take Berstow with me." He dragged him into a corner. "What have you done?" Jerome did not answer. "I want to hear what you were doing with that criminal over there," hissed Conrad. He sounded each word while pointing at Garnett.

"I don't want to talk," Jerome said with a low voice.

"But you're going to!" shouted Conrad so loud that he could have been heard even outside the building. "And I want to hear the truth, damn it! I'm entitled to it." He made sure his tone promised the worst. "Let's start with what you were doing with Mr. Garnett."

"They needed me for some wiring," Jerome said finally.

"Who are they? And what kind of wiring? For what?" Jerome's eyes widened but he did not answer. "Wiring what, I asked, a chandelier in a ballroom?" Conrad paused. "How long did you work

191

for them?"

"About ten weeks. At the beginning it was the usual stuff. House wiring, computer equipment, a satellite dish, that sort of thing." For a split second Jerome looked into Conrad's eyes. Then his eyes shifted away and his Adam's apple began bouncing up and down.

Conrad was getting sick. "Keep talking," he ordered.

"They promised me—" Jerome started to cry. "They said they'd give me...that I'd get...." He burst into tears. "I would get...."

"A term in jail. That's what you'll get!" Conrad paused again and said, "How could you do something like that to yourself? To your mother?" Jerome did not utter a sound, his body trembling. "Stop shaking, and start singing, do you hear me?" Jerome nodded. "The truth, now. Then I'll see what I can do for you. But I want the entire truth. This means details, Jerome."

"Yes, yes. But I didn't do anything wrong! I mean, I did what they asked me to do. I bought some electronics for them. Small stuff: timers, amplifiers...it's for a big house in the hills...."

"Who are *they*?"

"I worked for Mr. Donavan. For Fred Kusteroff too."

"Ron Donavan?" shouted Conrad. Jerome nodded. "What was Ron Donavan doing there?"

"Weeks ago he set up a generator, because there are no power lines close to the house. Then he found out that it wasn't powerful enough. So he had to buy a new one, and redo all the hookups. That's when he asked me for help. But he got sick."

Sick? The man was on the run; that's why they had asked Jerome to take over. More pieces of the puzzle were falling into place. Chances were, the house where they had been taking Jerome to work was Todd's. "The house, where is it?"

"Branch off Highway 62. About ten miles on Road 57. Turn on a gravel road. South, I believe. But I always went there at night. After the turn, five or six miles. On a bumpy trail, no normal road."

Instantly, Conrad made a sign to Rudy Ashwald and told him to get ready for a raid on what could be Todd's hideout.

Jerome's face contracted with spasms when he said aloud, "Mr. Tormez, I did not want to go back to the house this last time. You have to believe me, Mr. Tormez. It's God's honest truth."

"Why didn't you want to go back last time?"

The young man turned his face away from Conrad. "I found out...."

Conrad pulled Jerome's face straight and gave him his famous cross-eyed look.

Jerome shook harder, his face contracted by convulsions. He hesitated then looked at him, a plea in his voice. "There were working with explosives, that's why they needed timers."

Conrad shook Jerome's shoulders. "Explosives? You mean they were making bombs?" Jerome nodded, then he nodded once again, much harder.

"Do you know where these bombs are located?"

"Somewhat."

"Think hard, Jerome. It's a question of life or death."

"One is in the basement, the other two are on the main floor." The young man closed his eyes, trying to concentrate. "Rooms at the opposite sides of the house. Let me think. Left and back, getting in from the main entrance. The other is to the right and at the front. One alarm on the main entry." He opened his eyes. "Will I go to jail?"

Conrad waved off his question. "How big or strong are the charges?"

"I don't know exactly; they were in boxes. The biggest could be seven to eight inches all around. Mr. Tormez? How...how much time do you think I'll get?"

Conrad glanced at the young man—he looked so much like his mother. He shook his head, more hurt than angry. "We'll see," he said.

He called for an officer and asked him to take Jerome away.

* * *

Near Barnist, The Rockies

Life in the bush was not much fun, Ron Donavan mused; yesterday he had burned the last few pieces of wood he had found behind the cabin. The skies were clear; the days were still short; and the valley, carved against Mount Maudit, got hardly any sun. He had to refurnish his log supply or freeze to death. With an ax and a rope, Donavan crossed the narrow valley and headed for the woods. He looked up to choose a tree that would not be too difficult to cut yet not too small. He found a dead pine of medium size leaning toward the clearing. He quickly swung the ax to cut a wedge on that side. He turned to the opposite side and began chopping with energy. When he stopped to have a rest, a noise attracted his attention. A helicopter circled high and retreated behind the mountains. A few moments later another appeared and repeated the maneuver. *Tourists: there were always tourists stupid enough to pay good money to see that big piece of ice that covered a large portion of Mount Maudit.* Donavan shrugged and went back to work. Soon the pine tree fell. He chopped a big piece out of it, put a rope around it, and began dragging it toward the log house: the rope, tight on his shoulder, almost cut through his leather coat.

He was halfway across the valley when the first helicopter appeared again, followed by the second, this time aiming at the clearing in front of the cabin. They touched ground: one near him, the other near the cabin. Donavan was puzzled. What were two helicopters doing in that forsaken place? He froze. For a moment nothing moved, then the door of the farther chopper opened and two men quickly took shelter behind the aircraft, two automatics pointed at him. From the nearer chopper two policemen dressed in black descended. One kept his hand near his belt, the other held a cellular.

Donavan let the rope go; with a big splash of snow the wood tumbled onto the ground.

The two officers stopped a few feet from him. "Mr. Al Garnett?" one asked.

"No," Donavan babbled.

"And who would you be?"

Donavan felt lost. "Ron Donavan," he mumbled.

"Would you come with us, please?" the first policeman asked. The second, meanwhile, stepped aside and punched a few keys on his cellular.

Conrad was in his office when he received that call. "The man denies being Al Garnett and claims to be Ron Donavan? He may be telling the truth! We got Al Garnett two hours ago. My men searched Donavan's house and farm, and found some interesting chemicals, carefully camouflaged as farming supplies. For the moment you can book him on possession of explosives. But we're gathering evidence that he was building bombs. We'll send you a fax with the details."

Conrad rubbed his hands together. Another of Todd's key men had fallen into the net. He would celebrate if not for the fact that Todd was holding Savina and Denis.

To outsmart Todd he needed a brainstorm and a cosmic amount of luck.

42

It was eight o'clock at night, too dark to attempt a raid at Todd's place. They would have to wait for daybreak. Conrad kept planning. He called upon a team specializing in explosives, sketched a plan of Todd's residence according to Jerome's description, and jotted down a few ideas on how to penetrate Todd's hideout and rescue Savina and Denis. He stayed on the phone for more than two hours, analyzing with his colleagues every minute detail of the upcoming operation—he wanted to be sure everything was ready for the following morning.

Seated on the floor in front of the TV set, Isabel watched *Shrek* for the second time. She danced in place to the rhythm of *My Beloved Monster*. Bobo lay on the mat near the door, waiting for Conrad. Bernice kept busy with her quilt, wondering at times about Jerome and at other times about Conrad, who, she had been told, was well but involved in a complex operation. She got two pieces of fabric out of her sewing basket and cut the blue material in small squares of equal size. She superimposed a paper pattern on the white fabric and cut flowers out of it. White on blue would make a beautiful color combination for Conrad Junior's quilt. She worked on a square, then on another, hoping to appease her anxiety. She looked at her wristwatch—eleven thirty! She waited for the movie to finish, then told Isabel to go upstairs and to bed. She wanted to be alone with Conrad when he got home.

At one o'clock in the morning, Conrad left the station. On the way home he wondered how he would break the news about Jerome's arrest. It wasn't going to be easy, since he was always the one who calmed Bernice's anxieties about her son's behavior. *She had been right to be worried!* he admitted to himself.

Bernice was still up. As he took off his shoes and tossed his coat on the entry rack, Conrad glanced at her, then slowly walked to the middle of the room.

Bernice stopped stitching, rose and approached Conrad. "What happened? I called the station several times; they told me you were okay, but too busy to come to the phone."

With a familiar gesture, Conrad took Bernice's arms and looked into her eyes. "They caught Jerome. He was driving a stolen vehicle." Bernice's eyes widened. She put a hand on her mouth, as if bracing for worse. "If that wasn't enough, there were stolen goods in the truck," Conrad said gravely.

He walked toward the living room couch, always holding Bernice's arms. They both sat, close to each other. "There will be charges against him," Conrad said.

"I knew something was wrong," she said as tears welled in her eyes. "At the beginning, there was that cab coming and going, especially late in the evening; then recently, a bundle of hundred dollars bills under the mattress!" Tears began raking her face. "Will he go to jail?"

"He *is* in jail, right now. But if you're asking me whether he'll serve time, the answer is no. I mean, I don't think so. He's cooperated without hesitation and exhaustively. I think he told us everything he knew. And I believe they tricked him into working for them. The judge will go easy on him—at least let's hope so." He caressed Bernice's short hair and kissed her on the cheeks. "I need a couple of hours to rest," he said, and rose. "Today we got a lead on where to find Savina and Denis. I spent the last few hours at the station thinking of a number of scenarios to get them back unharmed."

43

It was the crack of dawn. With an agile move Conrad Tormez jumped in the back seat of a police car. "Go," he shouted to the driver. A message came over the radio that the rescue squad was on its way.

The cruiser rushed toward Kurt Todd's refuge in the middle of the hills, eighty miles away.

His long-term enemy had eluded him for long weeks, and now he was holding Savina and Denis. They were probably confined in Todd's house, which was wired with explosives. Todd had a high-value bargaining chip in his hands. He would use it, Conrad was sure of that, and he would use it to his full advantage.

This is a matter of life or death, Conrad thought in a flash.

He ordered the driver to stop at the foot of the escarpment, a thousand feet from Todd's house, so that they would be shielded from any firing. The second police car joined them, its tires squealing as it came to a full stop. The third skidded a few feet on the snowy ground and lined up with the others. Within a few minutes, the sound of vanes became distinct. A helicopter landed behind the barrier formed by the cruisers.

Three men wearing uniforms flecked with brown and green spots got off the helicopter. Each had a huge backpack and an automatic. This was the rescue squad Conrad had called for.

"Nick, Sir, the team leader. Specialist in explosives. Detonation systems, contact or remote, sound, infrared, you name it."

"Dave, Sir. Trained in penetration: ducts, sewage, any opening one can think of. And a few others I can dig up myself, if necessary."

"Mike, Sir. I'm a specialist in acquiring data by way of optical and electronic instruments."

Nick gestured his men to line up behind him. "Mr. Tormez, on the phone you spoke of explosive charges and hostages. How many?"

"Three charges, two hostages." Conrad gave them the sketch he had drawn the night before. "The charges are located in the spots marked in red."

"By any chance, do you have the house blueprints?" Nick asked.

"Nope," Conrad replied.

Nick seemed to think aloud. "Big house. Three thousand, no, thirty-two hundred square feet. Front resting on four pillars. A steep path leading to the main entry. A staircase on the south side. Any other feature of importance?" he asked his crew.

"A skylight on the north side of the roof," said Dave promptly.

Nick nodded. "We'll gather more information with our optical instruments as we approach the target. Anything else you want to tell us?"

"I'll try to gain time by talking or whatever means I can think of to give you time to enter the house and defuse the charges."

"Great," Nick said. He slipped his backpack on his shoulders and briefly talked to his crew. In no time the three men were on their way to Todd's house, squeezing between rocks, bushes, and the few remaining clusters of snow, their stomachs grazing the highs and lows of the terrain.

Everybody was in tactical position, nervously watching the house. There was no sign of life.

Conrad was ready to use the loudspeaker, when a message was paged to him via the police station.

"This is Kurt Todd. I'd like to talk to Chief Detective Conrad Tormez."

Conrad grabbed the microphone. "This is Conrad Tormez."

The voice, speaking at a high pitch, continued, "Kurt Todd here. Surprised?"

"Not really."

"We meet again. You never stopped looking for me, right?" He paused and laughed. "One day I got fed up seeing you or your men wandering around my place. I tried to get you, but instead of you, I shot your partner and his wife. Uncertainty of the job!"

Conrad frowned. The motive for the murder of Savina's parents had always been a mystery, since the sniper had left no trace and no clues. At last the sniper had a name, and a face—the face of hatred.

"Now you know everything about me," Todd continued. "Surprised that I got your stunt girl, Savina? You camouflaged her well to look like my girl, Clara, Conrad. And I tip my hat to your discovery of a way to make her speech sound like Clara's. It was perfect. Too bad you didn't warn her how dangerous I am."

I did, and many times over! "You're only moderately dangerous," Conrad lied. *Never let an enemy know your real feelings or thoughts,* was Conrad's motto. "The game isn't over yet," he added in an even tone.

"Playing cool, eh?" said Todd, laughing hysterically. "In a moment this place could get hot, very hot. The entire house is wired."

Only in three places, thought Conrad. Jerome had been very precise.

"I'd like you to take a look at my two guests," said Kurt.

Savina and Denis were brutally pushed outside through the main door.

"So—" said Conrad. From that distance he couldn't see whether Savina and Denis were in good shape. A rope crossed their chests and, from the way they moved, they seemed to be tied together. Thank God they were both alive.

"Do you want them back?"

"I wouldn't mind," replied Conrad, coolly. The three specialists, now behind the cedars flanking the house, had reached their target, and were looking for points of entry. He should gain time. Time was going to be a big factor. The biggest of all. The one that could prevail. Because whatever game Kurt had in mind wasn't one Conrad was anxious to play.

"Want to know the price?" Kurt Todd asked.

"Sure," replied Conrad. One man was entering the house through a side window. "Sure," he repeated.

"A simple exchange." Kurt paused. "Savina and Denis for Conrad Miguel Tormez." He laughed, hysterical again. "You're lucky. Double the value, you see."

A freezing feeling went through Conrad, head to toe. So that's what it was. Revenge. Old, sweet revenge. He watched a second man enter the house through the same lateral window.

"You come here, unarmed, or I'll kill your friends this very instant," yelled Kurt. "This very instant," he repeated, fury in his voice.

Conrad searched for an escape. There wasn't any. Letting Savina and Denis die was worse than his own death. The third man was wandering on the roof, tiptoeing toward the skylight.

"The exchange," said Conrad slowly, "has to be fair. At the halfway point we are all three vulnerable."

Kurt Todd laughed aloud. "That's the idea. You have to trust me. We have to believe that I want to have a talk with you before blowing you up. A long talk, I mean." Conrad did not answer. "You come in now or I'll pull the trigger," screamed Todd. He pushed Savina and Denis further, keeping them leashed with the rope he had in his hand. In the other he held an automatic.

Conrad had to gain more time. In a calm tone he said, "Just a couple of minutes." Then serenely, almost hieratically, he added, "You call me to die. I need to get a grasp on my soul. A few minutes only." He made the sign of the cross, knelt and looked up, his hands joined in prayer. He watched the man on the roof lift the skylight glass and enter the attic.

He was ready now. He took his gun out of the holster and gave it to Rudy Ashwald.

"Ready," he shouted. "Free Savina and Denis."

Todd let the rope go.

Conrad started to walk, measuring his steps with Savina's and Denis'.

They met halfway. Conrad squeezed his eyes in a quick sign of greeting.

Adrenaline poured into Conrad's bloodstream; his muscles tensed in awareness of danger. His old wound began to ache, sending sparks of pain into his upper leg and back. Conrad kept going, limping at times. He had been in treacherous situations many times over, but he had never walked unarmed toward a killer, into a house ready to explode. He began to shake. Maybe he should attempt running. He looked up. Kurt Todd, his mouth semi-open in a grin of tension and amusement, held him in his scope. No chance. Todd, alias Dale Vernon, was the best shot in his class. His ability had probably improved, mused Conrad, with all the occasions he had to practice.

As he felt a minor pressure in his chest, Conrad slowed down.

He thought of the million things he should have done and did not, and the zillion he had done and shouldn't have. Looking back, he realized he should have prayed for real—his soul could use an ultimate, desperate appeal to the Almighty.

When he approached the entrance, he stopped for a second.

"Don't try any tricks. Move!" Todd shouted.

He entered the house. As Todd checked him for weapons, Conrad looked at him. Kurt was pale and skinny, and much taller than he remembered.

Todd gestured Conrad to a chair before him while he sat on a stool beside the front window. Todd's deep blue eyes moved fast, scrutinizing the room, outside, Conrad, back to the room, outside, and Conrad again. A black box with an On/Off switch hung on Todd's neck, kept in place by a double-looped cord.

"Your leg hurts, I noticed," Todd said with a grin of satisfaction. "Because of my shot, still?"

"Yes," replied Conrad. The memory of that fatal day flooded back, ancient and unwanted, but as vivid as ever.

The three of them—Al Garnett, Dale Vernon, and Conrad Tormez—had spent hours under a bridge, waiting for the fifty-pound bags of heroin to change hands.

It was a very cold afternoon; the sky had a lunar clarity and the wind whipped their faces. When the suspects showed up to make the grab, Conrad rushed out to arrest them. He had taken only a few steps when Al Garnett punched him in the face and sent him rolling in the mud. He had taken a long time to wrestle Garnett, since the man was a giant; but finally Conrad's agility and strength had prevailed. It was when he had gotten Garnett face down in the ground that Vernon stood in front of him and fired at his leg.

Instinctively, Conrad stretched his hand to touch the old wound.

With great effort, Conrad shoved aside the memory of that fatal day and the pain that came with it. He needed to be alert, and get a grasp on his environment. Unfortunately Todd had positioned him in such a way that the rising sun fell directly in his face, making him squint.

"You made a criminal out of me when—" started Kurt.

Conrad perceived a light tapping from the basement, where the biggest charge was located. He coughed a couple of times, trying to cover up the noise.

Kurt, alert, rose to look outside. He came back and sat back on his stool. He continued, "You made a criminal out of me when you disclosed my involvement with Mr. Mob."

"And exposed you as the man who shot his partner—me—in the course of an action in which all your associates should have been apprehended," finished Conrad. He coughed again, louder this time. "You were already a criminal, even though you were serving on the force."

Todd's voice was shrill when he replied, "You weren't supposed to be there, damn it! I tried to send you home." He paused. "You could have it easy," he added with nostalgia. "You ruined me, making me hide for the rest of my life. I'll never forgive you. Killing you is now more important than living."

There was a sharp noise, like the fall of a metallic object.

"You fucking bastard! You have a man inside!" Kurt jumped to his feet and moved away from the window. "Up! Get up!" he yelled. "Walk in front of me." With his gun he pushed Conrad down the stairs.

Nick had done his job, thought Conrad. A variety of tools were spread on the floor. No charge was in sight.

"Shit! I'll get mean with you. I'll make you cover for my escape. Then I'll blow you up." He pushed Conrad toward another room on the same floor. Neatly arranged, weapons and tools of all sorts hung from the walls. Wires in various boxes, each with an ID tag, were stacked on a shelf. Todd picked up a leather belt with a big buckle; near the buckle was a piece of paper with the word *cellular*.

While Todd was busy fiddling with the belt, Conrad tried to take off. He slid toward the nearest wall and grabbed a wrench. He was turning toward Todd when the man reached him in two big steps and hit him over the head with the stock of his gun. Conrad fell to the floor. Todd did not lose any time. While Conrad was down, he put the belt around Conrad's waist and locked it in place. He exchanged the black box around his neck with what looked like a normal mobile phone. "Done," Todd said with exhilaration.

Conrad's head was hurting and his vision blurred, but even so he managed to follow Kurt's moves. "Done what?' he asked.

"You're wearing a nice long-range trigger system," Kurt replied, excited. "A current flows in the belt you're wearing. The charge inside the buckle blows up if I dial the right number or if the current stops. Effective, since it discourages people from taking off the belt and getting loose." He paused. "I can activate this system at any distance with a simple phone call." He forced Conrad to stand. "I'm going to show you how smart I am before I blow you into a hundred pieces." He pushed Conrad up the stairs and toward a lateral door. He opened it and kicked Conrad outside and toward the stairway handrail. "Look at the courtyard below," he said. "What do you see?" Todd stayed inside, scouting around as if he was looking for something.

"A car," answered Conrad, "and a heap of logs."

"Anything else?"

Conrad squeezed his eyes to look better. Moving cautiously, Nick was heading toward the rock at the back of the house. He carefully deposited a box on the left side of the logs. "Nothing of importance," Conrad said evenly. "Except for the car. A white car."

"Look better. Looked where it's parked," said Todd, grabbing a sports bag.

"Parked with the hood against the wood logs, which are piled up against the rock," Conrad said. "Ready to go nowhere."

Nick gave him the okay sign, followed by the sign three. The three charges had been taken care of. Nick retreated and walked toward the stairway where Conrad was standing. He hid underneath it.

"Those logs are my escape!" Todd said loudly while packing his bag. "They are nothing but a doorway that opens onto a tunnel. That tunnel will take me to the other side of the hill while everybody will be busy looking for my carbonized body." He laughed hysterically. "At the end of the tunnel I have another car. Smart, eh?" He looked at Conrad with an air of victory. "I'll disappear, as I did in the past." He zipped the bag shut and joined Conrad on top of the stairs. "It'll take at least fifteen minutes to defuse the bomb you're carrying in your belt. Before then I'll dial the fatal number and you will be history. While I...I'll be traveling on Highway 135 on the other side of the tunnel. On the loose, and free as a bird." He laughed again.

Todd briskly descended the stairs and began walking backward. His eyes scouted around and his gun pointed toward the house. He reached the white car.

Conrad murmured to Nick, "Todd has only a cellular to control the explosive in my belt. Take him."

A rapid sequence of shots filled the air.

Kurt arched backward, his mouth opened in a spasm of pain. His left hand fumbled to reach the phone keypad.

Nick fired again, this time hitting the stack of logs.

Kurt's body had only touched the ground when a burst of flames shrouded the logs, followed by a blast. The white car flew high in the air, to fall back in myriad pieces. Debris seemed to come from everywhere while the house walls jiggled like jelly.

Then there was no more escape car, no more fake door to the tunnel, and no more Kurt Todd.

It was all over.

44

The old, heavy drawer did not budge; so Norman pulled on it once more, and harder. With a squeak the drawer gave way, sending Norman to the floor and covering him with ribbons, wrapping paper, and bows.

"Dangerous place you live in!" he shouted as Theresa lifted the old drawer from his chest.

"This is the only piece of furniture I shipped from my old apartment in Quebec City." She carefully deposited the drawer on top of the dining table. She fingered the inlays of ivory, featuring the Austrian two-headed eagle. "It's beautiful. It belonged to my grandmother—the one of the strudel recipe." She helped Norman free himself from the contents of the drawer. "There are still stamps!" she said aloud, surprised. "I thought I got them all." She picked up three stamps and spread them on the palm of her hand.

"Oh," said Norman feigning ignorance, "I didn't know you collected stamps."

"I don't, really. From time to time I save a few, but only if they look beautiful." She paused. "Maria Theresia, my late aunt, however, was a collector. She lived all her life in a village near Krems." She paused and smiled as she remembered. "You should see the village! The houses are small with steep roofs and cute little windows. On the windowsills are flowers of every kind and color. The streets are neat, some still hand-paved with stones of different sizes; in the main square stands a little church, built five hundred years ago. People don't rush, they seem to have time for each other. The place looks like...how should I say? Like it is out of time." Theresa turned to face Norman. "But let me go back to my aunt. She left all she had to me. Her house went to the bank, since it was heavily mortgaged. But the stamps turned out to be worth a pile of money. At least it was a huge amount for me, who never had any. They were from all over the world, but mostly from the Austrian-Hungarian Empire."

Norman's ears pricked with attention. He rose and went to sit on the sofa. "Theresa, come sit beside me, and tell me more about your aunt and the stamps. It's an intriguing story."

Theresa complied. "I received this big upholstered envelope—a mail cushion, it's called. Inside, there was a note from my aunt, and a million loose stamps. A draft from the open window sent the stamps flying all over the room. I tried to catch them all, but it was difficult. Days later I still found some in the most incredible places, hanging on or even in my clothes." She paused. "They often still have glue on their backs, so they stick wherever they go." She turned the three stamps in her hand. "Like this, for instance," she said lifting one of them.

Theresa set the stamps on top of the corner table. "I was already in contact with my aunt's lawyer, so I asked him if he could help me with their sale. He was happy to do so; he was an old friend of hers."

"Did you get any money?"

"Did I! I never figured out little pieces of paper could have so much value! It took me some time to have them appraised, but a few were very valuable." Theresa fingered her nose. "You may not believe what I'm going to tell you: I did not always look like this. I always had a nice figure, but my nose was too big, I wore thick glasses, and my teeth were crooked—not one lined up with the next! I used the stamp money to improve my looks. I disappeared for a while, going from one doctor to another in order to get the cheapest rate."

Norman bent to kiss her on every inch of naked skin he could find.

Theresa tried to free herself and asked, "What's the matter with you?'

"Nothing." He couldn't tell her how many times he regretted she was a con artist. *But she wasn't!* "It was worth the suffering and the money, Theresa. You look great. I'm always proud to take you places, and I enjoy looking at you." He began kissing her again.

Theresa threw her head back, shaking her soft red hair. "Maybe you should stop here, or you risk proposing."

Norman had found a girl to care for. She was honest, and so he was going to be. "But I will, Theresa. I want to spend my whole life with you."

Theresa looked down. "You don't even know my age."

"And that would be?" Norman asked, holding her chin up.

"Thirty-eight," she whispered. "There may be a problem if we want a family."

"Do you want kids?" Norman asked.

"Of course, I'd like them. But there isn't much time," she said, her voice wavering.

"Then we should start working on it soon." Norman kissed her again. "What about right now, Theresa?"

45

The last two weeks had been frantic. For a change Conrad looked forward to doing manual work. He got out his toolbox, a few pieces of plywood, and a saw. The backyard fence was in urgent need of repair, and this was the best time to do it, since Bernice had gone out with Isabel, Junior, and the dog. For a couple of hours he could work undisturbed.

As be began cutting the plywood to size, his mind wandered to the events of the previous weeks. It bothered him that Savina and Denis had not called. They were at the Caribbean retreat, he had been told. Clearly they had not been happy with the consequences of Operation Woman in Black. He may have lost their friendship; maybe they would never speak to him again. He shouldn't have asked innocent people to risk their lives to satisfy his thirst for justice. He should have known better.

He would have to be happy with the big headlines he had received from the press: "Conrad Tormez Does It Again," "Tormez Risks His Life To Save Hostages," "Conrad Captures Dangerous Criminals," "Not One Cop Injured in Action," and so on. In several ways and forms he was praised for the brilliant operation and his outstanding courage. Conrad laughed inwardly. The operation became brilliant when events got out of hand. He had to adopt daring solutions to save lives, including his own. The personal courage—what a laugh! If they only knew how scared he was! The courage he displayed was only the result of lack of choices.

With force Conrad nailed the few last boards together. He collected his tools and looked with satisfaction at his handiwork. Now Bobo wouldn't be able to escape; nor would Junior, once he started to crawl.

The noise of an approaching car signaled that is family was coming home. He wondered how Jerome was adapting to the sentencing he had received: doing social work at the Varlee Rehabilitation Center.

He entered the house, promptly greeted by a yapping Bobo. Conrad hugged Isabel, kissed Bernice, and stood in front of Jerome. "So how was your first day?" Jerome had to do community service for three full months. That meant working eight hours a day doing all the chores he was asked to do. And taking orders was, for Jerome, the hardest thing of all.

Jerome stood in front of him, an unusually relaxed expression on his face. "Good. The people I'm working with are real nice. They make me feel like I'm one of them." He walked to kitchen shouting, "I'm starved!"

Things were settling down, Conrad thought. Everything was going better than he ever expected. He took Junior from Isabel's arms and went to sit in the rocking chair. He felt too young to be a grandfather, but he was extremely proud when he could show off such a beautiful baby as part of his family.

The phone rang, and Bernice took the call. She covered the mouthpiece and murmured to Conrad, "It's Savina, she wants to talk to you."

Holding Conrad Junior with one arm, Conrad grabbed the phone with the other. "Hello, Savina," he said cheerfully.

"Hi, Uncle. Denis and I want to thank you, immensely, for what you did for us, risking your life, and all that...."

"Happy to hear your voice, Savina," Conrad said simply.

"But, Uncle, I have to thank you for something else. You introduced me to a wonderful man. You know what he's going to do? He's going to take me around the world to see shows in big theaters in Paris, London, and Rome. He may even take me to the Bolshoi, he said. And all this because you asked me to play a certain part. Isn't it wonderful?"

Conrad could hear Savina laugh. It surely had been a big part, and they both knew it. He managed to keep the emotion out of his voice. "Yes, Savina. It's wonderful." He paused. "It's wonderful you remembered to call your uncle."

Other Books by Rene Natan

Cross of Sapphires

Chief Steve Carlton seems to have successfully carried out his mission—he has finally managed to take fugitive Livia White aboard his aircraft.

Shortly after take off, however, Steve's plane crashes in the wildest region of Venezuela. Severely injured, he is nursed back to health by an attentive and caring Livia. For five long weeks Steve tries to picture her as a killer. To no avail. Her limpid blue eyes, her rare but genuine smile, and her kindness capture his heart.

But when Steve returns to New Brunswick he discovers that the evidence accumulated against Livia is staggering. The law being his one and only creed, Steve battles his feelings as the life of accused Livia White unfolds before his eyes.

Follow Steve in his struggle and his adventures, where the stakes are high and the rewards none too sure.

Mountains of Dawn

Pack and leave are the words that Tanya Caldwell, orphaned at the age of six, heard many times over as she wandered from foster home to foster home. She hears them again from Malcolm Clark, the head of the prestigious agency Invicta, after she narrowly escapes two murder attempts.

On Malcolm's advice, she retires to the hills of the Riviera.

The Mediterranean shores offer endless inspiration to Tanya the artist. Here she meets Kevin Matwin, a publisher of arts books, and a friend of his, Luigi Amedeo, Count of Monteturro. The count's dignified manners and his daredevil enterprises hide more than one secret.

Accidents similar to Tanya's also occur to Brian, Malcolm's brother. Because Tanya's and Brian's misfortunes have a common denominator in a...

The Collage

A cleverly masterminded plot entraps young heiress Allison Summer in a web of deceit and violence--slowly but without mercy. Even if surrounded by a multitude of people, beautiful Allison is alone in her struggle, not knowing whom to trust: not her father, not her husband, not even the handsome man who pledges his love to her...

A nosy reporter makes Allison's life difficult, a mysterious fire destroys her home, a killer seemingly coming from nowhere knocks on her door, while an accusation of murder hangs over her head.

Overcome by guilt and disheartened by the loss of loved ones, Allison suffers in solitude, hoping for better times. But when the life of the man she loves becomes at stake, Allison musters her strength and takes control of her destiny. And she will not stop until the innocent is free and the guilty secured behind bars.

Printed in the United States
36689LVS00004B/184